M000045993

FALLING FOR PRINCE FEDERICO

NICOLE BURNHAM

Royal
Scandals
San Rimini

Falling for Prince Federico

by Nicole Burnham

Copyright © 2004, 2020 by Nicole Burnham

This book is a work of fiction. Names, characters, places, and incidents are either products of the author's imagination or used fictitiously. Any resemblance to actual events, locales, or persons, living or dead, is entirely coincidental.

All rights reserved. No part of this publication can be reproduced or transmitted in any form or by any means, electronic or mechanical, without express permission in writing from the author or publisher.

Cover design by Patricia Schmitt

Edition: June 2020

ISBN: 978-1-941828-49-6 (paperback)

ISBN: 978-1-941828-48-9 (ebook)

ISBN: 978-1-941828-50-2 (audio)

For more information or to subscribe to Nicole's newsletter, visit nicoleburnham.com.

CHAPTER 1

"I'M NEVER GOING to be able to tell a placenta previa from a placenta accreta."

Pia Renati reminded herself to keep her grumbling under her breath, then leaned one shoulder against the backlit cologne ad adorning the wall of the San Rimini International Airport and flipped to the next page of a thick, floral-jacketed pregnancy guide. How in the world did women have babies without a medical degree?

And why in the world had *she* gotten the call when her friend Jennifer Allen—now Jennifer diTalora—needed someone to come stay with her during her obstetrician-imposed bed rest?

Pia's friends always looked to her in a disaster. As Pia's former boss at the refugee camp where they'd worked a little over two years ago, Jennifer knew that better than anyone. Setting up food banks came as naturally to Pia as walking. Helping to build temporary housing under a hot African sun? Establishing databases to reunite those fleeing conflict with their loved ones? Been there, done that. As a relief worker, Pia didn't fear hard work, and she'd been around more than one field hospital. But caring for a pregnant woman due to deliver the newest heir to San Rimini's throne at any time? What Pia knew about pregnancy and kids she'd learned in the last hour.

Her own mother hadn't exactly emulated the warm and loving maternal types that were standard issue on television sitcoms. Even most cartoon mothers would have been an improvement over the perpetually-absent Sabrina Renati. But Jennifer insisted she wanted Pia by her side, and Pia wasn't about to say no to a pregnant friend who happened to be married to the crown prince of Pia's home country.

Pia skipped to the next section of the pregnancy guide that Jennifer had sent her, nearly dropping it on the floor of the crowded airport terminal when faced with a full-page black-and-white photo of a woman giving birth. She'd assumed the book would leave certain moments to the imagination.

Well, she supposed, the shot could have been in color.

"Signorina Renati?"

Pia barely heard the smooth baritone behind her, since at that exact moment the airport's public announcement system loudly requested a passenger report to security for a lost item.

Instead, a sudden sense of foreboding made Pia snap the book shut. The hum of conversation around her ceased and every single set of eyes on the concourse focused on the man behind her.

Without turning around, Pia realized who had to own the distinctive, opera-caliber voice. It wasn't a palace driver as she'd expected, coming to show her the way to his Volkswagen minivan, but quite arguably the world's most desired single male, the recently widowed Prince Federico Constantin diTalora. The man known by tabloid readers everywhere as Prince Perfect for his Mediterranean good looks, unimpeachable reputation, and his devotion to duty.

Of course. The one time she didn't get the chance to grab a breath mint or fix her makeup before getting off an overnight flight.

Hoping he hadn't been surveying her reading material over her shoulder, Pia forced herself to smile as she turned to face Jennifer's brother-in-law, the man second in line to the thousand-year-old throne of San Rimini.

Judging from the expression on his oft-photographed face, the prince had gotten a good look at the photo in the book.

It had been years since she'd been home and able to speak her native San Riminian-accented Italian, and Pia had been anxious to chat with someone who understood her heritage. Someone who could discuss San Riminian politics, give her the latest gossip about local celebrities, maybe update her on the newest restaurants and hole-in-the-wall dance clubs.

But the sight of the famous royal—a well-toned man who filled out his understated black suit and crisp white shirt as well as any action star walking the red carpet at the Academy Awards—took her aback, and she only managed to get out a feeble, "Prince Federico. *Buon giorno. Come sta?*"

What in the world was he doing here? Jennifer never mentioned sending Federico to the airport. The prince not only towered over Pia, he possessed that intangible quality that every man coveted—charisma. They'd been introduced during Jennifer's wedding to Crown Prince Antony two years earlier, and Pia had been so nervous she'd said the required niceties and quickly retreated to the reception table where her co-workers from the Haffali refugee camp were seated, overwhelmed by the brief encounter.

Federico and his elegant wife, Lucrezia, were polite enough, but both seemed above the festive, romantic atmosphere of the wedding reception. Lucrezia had been everything Pia wasn't—tall, rail-thin, and golden, with dark, straight hair, full red lips and a sense of style worthy of catwalks. The type of woman every fashion editor clamored to have featured in their magazines.

And Federico? Well, his mere presence had intimidated the hell out of her. His quiet, composed demeanor, combined with his polished shoes, custom tuxedo, and royal sash had stolen her breath that night.

And then there were those amazing cheekbones. The strong, smooth jaw that never showed a hint of five o'clock shadow. The rich olive skin she imagined felt like heaven under a woman's fingertips.

Pia clasped the pregnancy book against her sage green cotton T-shirt and wished she'd thought to dress a notch above khaki pants and sandals. At least the last time she'd met Federico, she'd been wearing a designer gown and heels.

The prince made a subtle gesture with his right hand, and a lean man standing nearby rushed forward to pick up the bag at Pia's feet. "I am quite well, thank you. However, if you do not mind, I would prefer to converse in English. I am attempting to improve my skills, and do not often have the chance to practice with someone who speaks both our language and English so well. You have spent a great deal of time in the United States, yes?"

She held back a sigh. "I have, and English is fine."

While she would have preferred Italian for casual conversation, hearing the prince call her *signorina* made her feel like a kid, and less mature than her thirty-two years. It was a term used in San Rimini by her grandparents' generation. Besides, it wasn't as if the prince was the casual conversation type, anyway.

"Wonderful. I arranged for your checked bag to be delivered directly to the palace by the airline. Jennifer is anxious to see you, so if you are ready to depart, my car is waiting through here." He indicated a set of thick metal doors along the concourse wall. To the right, through the floor-to-ceiling windows, Pia noticed a shiny black Mercedes parked on the tarmac alongside the airplane from which she'd just disembarked.

The privilege of being a prince, she supposed. No need to battle for a parking spot, go through endless security checks, or wait for your suitcase alongside a hundred other tired travelers jockeying for position beside the baggage claim carousel.

The crowd parted in front of Federico as he led the way through the waiting area and out the gray metal doors. The second the prince's feet hit the stairway leading to the tarmac, the concourse buzzed back to life behind them. Travelers asked each other if the man they'd seen really was the prince, and if they knew who the woman was that he'd met.

Pia held the railing as she descended the stairs into the sunlight, forcing herself not to listen to the knot of gawkers forming near the windows. They'd be disappointed if they knew the truth. It was a relief when she heard the heavy security doors close behind her.

Pia glanced up at Federico as the driver opened the rear door for her, then realized that the prince was offering his hand to help her into the back seat.

"Oh. Thank you." Did she stick out like a goose among swans, or what?

She slipped her hand into his, and wasn't surprised to find his grasp solid, practiced. He must hand women into fancy cars every day. She ducked her head, praying she wouldn't smack it against the car roof, and hoped that he couldn't tell how jumpy his presence—let alone his touch—made her.

Once they were buckled into the sedan's baby-soft leather seats, the prince asked a few courteous questions about when she'd last visited San Rimini, what she thought Jennifer and Antony might name the baby, and whether the infant would be a boy or a girl, since Jennifer and Antony had opted not to find out. Pia managed to give some polite answers, but before they'd even exited the airport property, their conversation drifted off. He appeared perfectly content to ride along quietly, occasionally looking out the window on his side of the car. As the silence stretched on, Pia's nervousness only grew.

The drive to the royal palace was a scenic one, carrying them along the Strada il Teatro, San Rimini's main thoroughfare, which ran above the very northern coast of the Adriatic Sea. After passing the refurbished Royal Theater near the eastern end of the Strada, they'd climb up twisting, centuries-old cobblestoned streets to the top of a broad hill, where La Rocca di Zaffiro, the country's famous royal palace, overlooked the bustling casinos and quaint shops and homes of the tiny European principality.

Pia smiled to herself, happy to see that little had changed since her last visit. She often daydreamed of San Rimini Bay's azure waves lapping against the shore, the lights of the seaside casinos, and the glitz of the country's posh hotels. Her mouth watered at the mere thought of the decadent desserts and rich pasta and seafood dishes that made San Rimini a mecca for foodies. On the difficult days when working in dusty camps or overheated mess tents in war- or disease-ravaged areas lost its appeal, those daydreams about San Rimini put her soul at rest. She hadn't lived here since she was nineteen and left to attend college in the United States, but it was home, and she relished each moment of her infrequent visits.

Or, she would, if not for the fact she sat elbow-to-elbow with Prince Perfect, who remained silent. Suddenly, the short drive seemed like it would take an eternity.

But hadn't he said he wanted to practice his English? Perhaps her single syllable answers to his questions had turned him off, and he was too practiced at diplomacy to let it show.

Screwing up her courage, she tried to restart the conversation. "You know, it's hard for me to believe Antony and Jennifer are married, let alone that they're about to become parents."

The prince turned from the window and audibly cleared his throat, making her wonder if she'd said the wrong thing. When he replied, his words, spoken with an accent and in a tone far too serious for the topic, gave her no reassurance. "They are quite happy."

Pia forced herself not to shrink back against the leather seat. She knew that she constantly put her foot in her mouth, but this was all in her mind. He couldn't be as distant or as threatening as she imagined. He was human, right? A title didn't make him better than her. Besides, Jennifer had repeatedly described Prince Federico as a gentle, loving man, and royal gossip columnists raved about how much he loved his two young sons.

While those columnists weren't an ideal source of information, Jennifer wasn't the type to give false praise.

Perhaps, Pia reasoned, she had simply misread his aloof demeanor at the wedding. Entirely possible, given that they'd been introduced late at night, after Prince Federico had spent the entire day assisting his brother with various events prior to the ceremony. And perhaps the loss of his own wife on the heels of that wedding had changed him, made him suspicious of unmarried women—most of whom were probably trying to coax him into a romantic relationship.

If she'd married some beautiful, perfect spouse and then lost that person to an aneurysm at an early age, suddenly finding herself a young, single parent and the target of fortune hunters, she'd be a little reserved, too.

"Oh, I don't doubt they're happy, Your Highness." She shoved a blond curl away from her face, thankful that the humidity from the Adriatic couldn't make her hair look any worse than it already did after her long flight from Washington, D.C., and doubly thankful that she'd remembered to add the *Your Highness* when she spoke to him this time. "I only meant that it's hard for me to believe that Jennifer is about to become a parent. You have to understand, during the time I worked with Jennifer at the Haffali refugee camp, I watched her dig latrines, scrub mess tent floors, and climb hills in work boots carrying jugs of water in each hand. She's tough, and she cares about the people in her life. I'm sure you've been able to spend enough time around her to see that. But that doesn't exactly translate to stuffed bunnies and nursery rhymes. That's all I meant."

Federico smoothed the front of his suit jacket and nodded. "I see. Then I am glad Jennifer has found someone with maternal instincts to remain with her these next weeks before the baby's birth. I did not want her to be alone."

His expression was unreadable, his words lacking any hint of sarcasm. His sense of decorum wouldn't allow it. But if he only knew how little maternal instinct she had, he'd snatch the words back. After the lousy job her own mother had done raising her—or more accurately, not raising her—the last thing Pia wanted was to be anyone's mother. Jennifer would be a hundred times better at mothering than Pia.

"The palace has a sizable staff. And you're there, so she's not really alone. I know she has a lot of respect for you and the way you're raising your sons." To the best of Pia's knowledge, Federico didn't travel as often as his siblings, choosing to keep close to the palace for the sake of his boys.

"What you say about the presence of others is true, but I believe Jennifer would prefer the company of a woman. Someone who understands her, and who knows how to keep her spirit above it." He shifted in his seat, as if uneasy. "Is this the phrase in English?"

"Very close. I think you mean 'keep her spirits up.'"

"Yes. That is it. She might also wish for a friend to stay with her at the hospital, should her labor begin before Antony returns."

Pia tried to ignore what he had said about the hospital and the fact that his knee now brushed against hers, which was a surefire way to send her hormones into overdrive. Struggling to stay focused, she continued, "I'm surprised you didn't urge your brother to stay home with her."

A vertical crease appeared in the gap between his dark eyebrows. "Sometimes sacrifices are necessary to those in positions of power, Signorina Renati. We have duties our citizens expect us to perform. Those must come before any personal desires. Anyone who spends time in the royal household learns they must also follow that duty. And above all they must keep any" —he seemed to struggle for the correct word— "private matters of the palace confidential."

Ah. So that was the prince's real concern. Jennifer had stressed during the phone call that her bed rest was being kept out of the papers, at least for the time being. Prince Antony was in Israel, one of three nonpartisan mediators trying to hammer out a new territorial agreement. Jennifer didn't want the public to think less of him because he wasn't home with her, or for the delegates to worry that Antony might leave in the midst of their discussions. As much as the crown prince wanted to be by his wife's side during the final six weeks of her pregnancy, Jennifer and Antony knew that millions of people depended on his calming presence at the talks.

And Federico obviously worried Pia would be less than discreet.

She fought down her chagrin. She, of all people, understood the need to protect the peace, which the talks would hopefully accomplish. More than enough of her own life had been spent cleaning up the physical and emotional carnage of political clashes. Then again, she'd never held the opinion that one could raise children and save the world at the same time. Though she'd kept her concerns from Jennifer, Pia wondered how the couple would manage both their public role as members of an active royal family and their private role as parents.

The Mercedes rolled to a stop outside the palace's rear gate, moving ahead again after the guards ascertained the identities of the occupants. Pia leaned forward as much as her seat belt would allow, taking in the view of the royal rose garden and the stunning rear facade of the palace beyond. Through the open sunroof, she could hear children laughing somewhere nearby, enjoying the late summer weather and the warm breeze blowing off the Adriatic, and wondered if the sounds of merriment came from Federico's two sons.

She eased back in her seat, resisting the urge to peek out the window to identify the source of the happy noise. "Your Highness, you don't need to address me as *signorina*. I realize that it's still used occasionally, but it makes me feel…well, I'm not used to such formality. That being said, I do understand the need for discretion. Please don't be concerned about that. But tell me, if you were in Antony's position, would you stay and negotiate or come home to be with your family?"

Federico glanced out the window, as if he, too, had heard the children's laughter. "I am not in Antony's position. He is the crown prince and will someday lead this country. His obligations are different than my own."

"But if you were?"

"I would do as Antony is doing. It is necessary for the good of all." Federico straightened in the seat, moving his knee away from hers as he spoke. "At the moment, delegates on all sides of the table respect my brother and the work he has accomplished. That is an uncommon thing and could move the process along to the benefit of many, including the citizens of San Rimini. Jennifer understands that. And so will Antony and Jennifer's child, someday."

He spoke with such conviction that Pia found herself agreeing with him—for the most part. She couldn't help but admire his defense of his elder brother. Federico's elegant demeanor and expressive eyes mesmerized her, and whenever he spoke, the faintest smile touched his lips, as though he thought he could convince her of his arguments with nothing more than a gaze.

Given the contrast of his phenomenal baby blues against his olive skin, it probably worked on people nine times out of ten.

She smiled. "I understand the ramifications, Your Highness, and I admire Antony and Jennifer's dedication to duty. And, of course, the support you give them. But don't you think that when one becomes a parent—"

The crunch of gravel beneath the sedan's wheels and the approach of an older woman in a straight, woolen skirt gave the prince the opportunity to interrupt.

"Excuse me, Ms. Renati, but this is Harriet Hunt. She is Prince Antony's personal assistant and handles both Antony's and Jennifer's schedules. If you need anything during your stay at the palace, I am certain Ms. Hunt will be able to assist you."

The driver stopped at the base of the palace steps where the assistant waited, then he exited and strode to the rear of the vehicle to open the door for Pia and Federico. Once again, the prince offered his hand to assist her from the car. She shot him a smile of thanks and reminded herself not to get used to lavish treatment. She lived in hiking pants and trail shoes, not Armani gowns and Jimmy Choo heels.

Introductions were made, then Federico turned his attention back to Pia and gave her a curt nod. "I leave you in good hands. And once again, I do appreciate both your willingness to help and your discretion in this matter, as does my father, King Eduardo."

So that was it. A royal reminder to keep her mouth shut and a goodbye. Pia watched him take the wide stairs into the palace by twos, all the while maintaining his upright, proper posture and athletic grace.

Amazing.

She'd broached a topic far more personal than most would dare with a member of the royal family, yet it seemed to roll off him as if she'd mentioned nothing more contentious than the weather. Part of his upbringing, she guessed, that need to be able to hide one's emotions.

If she possessed half his sense of propriety, she wouldn't have prodded, but part of her needed to hear his response, to be assured of the fact that he believed his sons were more important than his job. That he did, in fact, experience emotion outside of his dedication to duty, and that the children whose laughter she'd heard on the way in to the palace grounds would continue their happy antics when they saw their father, and would know that they were more than just an heir and a spare, acting as royal placeholders until Antony and Jennifer became parents.

She hoped they knew that he loved them more than anything else on earth.

"Ms. Renati, a pleasure to see you again," the assistant interrupted Pia's thoughts, her crisp British accent sounding out of place in San Rimini. "We met briefly before Prince Antony's wedding. You helped me direct the florists working at the cathedral when they arrived at the same time as the Dutch royal family."

Pia tore her gaze away from Federico's retreating back and smiled at Harriet, whose efficiency had made the woman a trusted employee of Antony and Jennifer's. "How kind of you to remember. And please, call me Pia. After riding in that car with His Highness, I've had enough of formality."

"I understand. Federico adheres to proper etiquette even more than his father." Her tone was professional, but her eyes showed her amusement. As they waited for the driver to retrieve Pia's bag, Harriet added, "I've started to take special note of the Americans who come through our doors. They have a tendency to marry into the diTalora family."

"So I've heard." Amanda Hutton, who'd been Jennifer's maid of honor, had stayed on after the wedding as some kind of diplomatic employee at the palace. Pia didn't know Amanda well, but knew that Prince Marco, the youngest—and wildest—of the four diTalora siblings proposed to Amanda soon afterward. And Princess Isabella married an American only last month.

"Fortunately, that won't happen with me," Pia promised. "While I sound American, I'm San Riminian, and I'm only here to help a pregnant friend."

But as Harriet led her through the double doors at the rear of the palace, then through one ornate mirror- and art-bedecked hallway after another, Pia found her thoughts returning to Prince Federico. The smooth cotton of his starched shirt, the broad expanse of his shoulders, the protective set to his mouth when he talked about Antony and Jennifer.

When they passed by a portrait of Federico laughing with his father during a national parade, Pia decided that if the prince could learn to relax a little, act a little less like he lived life by a carefully drawn script, he might be worth getting to know. Perhaps, just perhaps, those women who mooned over the tabloid pictures of Prince Perfect were on to something.

Pia's hand instantly went to her stomach at the thought. What possessed her to think that? She wasn't that brave—she'd barely kept her composure while being helped into the back seat of a car by the man.

Okay. It had been a long, long time since she had been in a relationship. Her job didn't allow much flexibility on that front, and her job meant everything to her. So what if Prince Federico oozed confidence and turned heads with his quiet grace? He clearly didn't approve of her, and she didn't plan to give him a second look, either. Giving a man a second look would get her exactly where Jennifer was.

Enviable as most might find Jennifer's position, Pia had no intention of ever needing one of those floral-jacketed books for herself.

WHY HAD he given her a second look?

Federico diTalora stared out the window that topped the staircase leading to the wing that housed his family's private apartment. From this vantage point, he could see Harriet standing on the outdoor steps speaking with Pia Renati while the driver fetched the blonde's well-worn carryall from the back of the Mercedes.

She was a scruffy thing. Short, untamed curls everywhere. Outdoor sandals like nothing he owned. Clothes that were... what was the word? Hippie? No, she wasn't a hippie, not as he understood the term. But she was close.

Earthy. Real.

She bothered him. His initial impression of her, when she'd scurried away from him at Jennifer and Antony's wedding nearly eighteen months ago, made him wonder if high society unsettled her. He'd encountered that reaction more than once. The media made him, and others of the royal family, into something bigger than they really were. Untouchable. Perfect.

How he hated that word, *perfect.* Lucrezia's death taught him he was anything but.

Given her heritage, Pia should know nobility made mistakes. She might be a commoner, but if he recalled correctly, Viscount Angelo Renati—a friend of Antony's—was her first cousin. Angelo, with his reputation for womanizing, never had to worry about the tabloids calling him perfect. And if not through Angelo, then Pia's mother certainly could have taught Pia a thing or two about nobility, since Europe's upper crust made up the bulk of Sabrina Renati's clientele. It suggested that Pia's odd behavior around him meant something more.

He suspected that rather than being skittish around royalty, Pia had looked him over, seen right through his Prince Perfect exterior, and judged him unworthy.

Federico adjusted the heavy curtain for a better look as Pia followed Harriet up the rear stairs and into the palace. Once the women were out of sight, he dropped the velvet panel and turned away from the window. He should be thinking about his sons, and about the problems he was having with their nanny—the third since their mother had passed away. But he found himself wanting to return to his conversation with Pia.

He knew he'd chosen duty before love when he'd married Lucrezia. They had run in the same circles since childhood, had understood each other, had understood the nature of royalty and the need for princes to marry well and produce heirs. They hadn't been in love, but that had never bothered them.

At least, it hadn't bothered him until she'd passed away, and he'd understood the difference love made in the lives of his two brothers and his sister.

Lucrezia had died only two weeks after they'd witnessed Antony and Jennifer's starry-eyed exchange of vows. Ever since, Federico had wondered if his decision to obey his duty and marry into the San Riminian aristocracy had cheated Lucrezia out of finding a loving husband, the type of husband Antony was to Jennifer. When he'd voiced his concern to Marco—the youngest of his siblings—Marco had sworn up and down that Lucrezia had entered the marriage with her eyes wide open, and that Federico shouldn't feel an ounce of guilt, that he hadn't cheated her. Federico and Lucrezia made their decision, Marco had pointed out, and Antony and Jennifer had made theirs. Relationships were as unique as the individuals involved and shouldn't be compared.

Federico had nodded, not because he agreed, but to end the conversation. Lucrezia had been intelligent, beautiful, and articulate. Dozens of men would have married her for love, and she'd deserved that. A romantic, passionate love wasn't the same as a love grown out of respect and familiarity.

He hadn't loved her enough to marry her. He'd seen it in Lucrezia's eyes as the two of them watched Antony dance with Jennifer at their wedding reception.

He'd be damned if he'd cheat his children because he failed to love them wholeheartedly.

He walked down the second floor's main hallway, then turned into another, smaller hallway that led to his private apartment. The nanny situation bothered him. Had the women he'd hired been a disappointment because he hadn't researched them adequately? Had he failed to spend enough time with his sons to understand their needs?

He hadn't thought so. Paolo and Arturo were bright, loving children, and he adored sitting in on their music lessons or taking them on outings to local parks and museums. The boys' banter lifted his heart on the days when he questioned whether there was anything to his life outside his public duties.

But Pia's words—words no one else had dared speak to him— made him wonder.

No, he chastised himself. He was only feeling guilty because Pia Renati spoke freely, something he wasn't used to. The blonde was like no woman he'd ever met, but that didn't mean she was correct.

A squeal of pain that could only belong to Arturo, his seven-year-old, stopped Federico in his tracks. He glanced out the nearest window, then heard another cry and realized that the sound had emanated from his apartments. Though Arturo constantly hurt himself, like any boy nearing the ripe old age of eight, Federico jogged rather than walked along the marble-floored corridor. By the time he reached the guard stationed near the entrance to his private apartment, Federico could also hear little Paolo crying and the high-pitched voice of their frustrated nanny asking them to shush.

"Your Highness." The guard greeted him with a nod, then slid a glance toward the door of the living quarters.

"What has happened?"

The guard held up his palms. "I don't know, but I assume nothing serious. Signorina Fennini is inside."

Federico thanked the guard, then entered the apartment, making a beeline for the boys' playroom. In a serious situation, the nanny knew to summon the guard. She'd certainly had to do it before.

When Federico pushed open the playroom door, chaos greeted him.

CHAPTER 2

"Papa! Get him off me!" Arturo cried the minute he noticed Federico in the doorway.

An antique ceramic vase encircled Arturo's arm, and five-year-old Paolo was attempting to pull it off, his face white with fear for his older brother. Arturo yelled again for Paolo to stop pulling, that his hand might fall off, and, he added, "I'll bleed all over you!"

Behind them, the nanny held the phone to her ear and gestured for the boys to settle down. From what Federico could discern, she'd called for the assistance of the palace doctor in extricating Arturo's trapped hand. At least she was doing something useful and not chatting with her friends again.

Federico went to Paolo first. The little boy's face crumpled at the sight of his father, but Federico managed to ease him away from his older brother. As Paolo let out a choked sob, the prince turned to Arturo. "Sit down and place your arm on the floor. Do not hold it in the air."

Arturo instantly quieted and plopped his bottom on the hooked car- and airplane-patterned rug covering the playroom floor, his wide eyes silently begging his father for help.

"Good." Federico sat next to Arturo, then pulled Paolo onto one knee, trying to calm the little boy while testing the vase around Arturo's arm with his fingers. It didn't seem too tight, but he didn't want to pull on it, since Paolo's attempts had only agitated Arturo. "Can you move your fingers at all?"

Arturo nodded. "But I can't get my hand out, Papa."

"Your grandfather's doctor is on duty downstairs. He will come help you. You will be strong and wait patiently, yes?"

The little boy squared his shoulders, and Federico ruffled his hair. "Good." In a whisper, he added, "You will be a good example for your brother and future cousins if you continue to be so brave."

The nanny finished her phone call, then hurried to the center of the room, where Federico sat with the boys. She dipped into a quick curtsey. "*Mi dispiace,* Your Highness. I called for the doctor, so he's on his way. Arturo wanted to break the vase to free his hand, but I didn't think that was a good idea. It looks expensive."

"No, not if the doctor can get his hand out. Arturo could be cut by the broken pieces." Federico studied the pale green vase, recognizing it as one his late mother acquired on a trip to Turkey nearly twenty years before. It held great sentimental value, but he'd gladly sacrifice it for his son if necessary.

A moment later, the doctor arrived, and Arturo showed the older man his arm. "My soldier fell in, *Dottore,*" he explained, holding up his arm and the vase with it. "I didn't mean to get stuck."

The doctor, who'd been with the family since Federico was young, gave Arturo a look of mock chastisement. "You should not go sticking your fingers in where they do not belong, Arturo. But it is not a problem. Your Uncle Marco did much worse when he was young."

Arturo's eyes widened, while Paolo started to giggle.

"He did?" asked Paolo. "Uncle Marco was *bad*?"

Seeing the edge taken off the boys' panic, Federico released Paolo, then stepped away to allow the doctor to inspect his patient. He met the nanny's gaze and raised an eyebrow, indicating that she should follow him to the corner of the room.

"What happened, Mona?" he asked once out of the children's hearing.

The nanny had the good sense to look apologetic. "We were taking a walk through the gardens, Your Highness, when Arturo realized he'd lost his soldier. We headed back to the playroom to search for it, and before I realized what had happened, he'd stopped and put his hand into the vase. He said he'd dropped his soldier in there."

"Why was he anywhere near that vase? It belongs on a display pedestal near the entrance to my father's apartment. That is not the way to the gardens."

A red flush spread across the young woman's cheeks, and she began to fiddle with the hem of her gray T-shirt, which was short enough to reveal a wide strip of skin above her tight black pants whenever she moved. Not for the first time, he wondered at the so-called exclusive nanny service that had referred her. He'd been told that their training program included discussions on how to dress appropriately for outdoor play while still appearing neat and polished enough to fit into a formal household. Even after spending three months with his family, Mona didn't seem to comprehend the notion that her professional appearance mattered.

Casual clothes were fine. Belly-baring outfits were not.

She finally dropped the hem. "I do not know, Your Highness."

"You do not know how he came to be near King Eduardo's apartment? Or you do not know where he found the vase?" He tried to keep his voice from sounding harsh. He hated to hurt the young woman's feelings, but he wondered how closely she'd been watching Arturo. It wasn't the first time Mona lost track of him, and it simply wasn't safe for the young prince to wander the palace corridors alone. It would be too easy for him to wander into his father's offices and interrupt an important government meeting, or to leave the secured areas and lock himself outdoors.

Worse, he might bump into one of the tour groups allowed into the public rooms. Anything could happen to him then. He might be photographed, asked personal questions about his family, grabbed, or worse.

Much worse.

"Neither, Your Highness," Mona replied, nervousness filling her voice. "I was carrying Paolo, since he was tired from walking outside. Arturo was following right behind me, but when I turned around to ask him a question, he was gone. I thought he must have gotten distracted and taken a different route to the playroom, but when I arrived at your apartment, the guard said he hadn't seen him."

A wave of concern gripped Federico's gut. "And you did not alert the staff? Or call me?"

"Not long after I spoke with the guard, Arturo came around the corner, and he had the vase stuck on his hand." Her entire face had gone crimson now, and her eyes filled with tears. "I apologize. I know I should have called sooner, but I thought I should bring him into the apartment and attempt to get the vase off his arm. I promise, it won't happen again."

Federico bit back his frustration, trying to keep in mind that the nanny was new to the palace, and only nineteen herself. "All right, Mona. But please, in the future, be sure to keep the boys in your sight at all times. You're their primary protector when I'm away, and not everyone has pure motives where my children are concerned. If these incidents continue, we shall reconsider your employment here."

Mona nodded. "Yes, Your Highness."

"Thank you." His tone softened, and he added, "I appreciate that you are trying. If I can do anything to make your job easier, let me know."

She replied that she would, and at that moment, a yell erupted from both boys. The doctor held up the vase. "You see, Arturo? You needed to let go of the soldier if you wished your hand to be free."

Federico ran a hand over his face, a combination of relief and exasperation running through him. Arturo had been holding on to the soldier? How could the nanny not have realized it?

How could *he* not have realized it? What kind of father was he?

Arturo rubbed his hand, slowly massaging the reddened skin back to a healthy color, then looked up at the doctor. "How do I get my soldier back? I can't leave him in there!"

The doctor turned the vase upside down and shook it a few times, dumping the soldier into Arturo's upturned palm. "Like this. Now both of you boys be more careful, all right?"

They nodded, anxious to behave in front of their father, if not around the nanny. "Yes, *Dottore.*"

The doctor took a final look at Arturo's hand to ensure the boy hadn't suffered an injury, then smiled at Federico and took his leave.

Federico crouched in front of the boys. He might have bungled the task of freeing Arturo's hand, but he wouldn't allow the more serious aspect of the vase incident go without note. "Paolo, Arturo. What were my instructions to you?"

"Listen to Signorina Fennini," they said in unison.

"And?"

"Do. Not. Leave. Her. Sight."

"Correct." Federico focused on Arturo. "You disobeyed, yes?"

"Yes, Papa." The little boy raised his deep brown eyes to meet Federico's and tightened his fist around his soldier, as if afraid his father would take it away. "I promise not to do it again. Promise!"

"Then I shall take you at your word." He gave hugs to both boys, then turned to Mona. "I have a fundraising dinner to attend tonight for the University of San Rimini. If you need anything, I shall have my phone with me."

"I'll make sure Arturo is good," Paolo assured him.

"You are only responsible for yourself, Paolo. Your brother will be good on his own. He has promised." Federico made his way out of the playroom, stopping briefly to straighten a stack of the boys' books, then turned at the door to give his sons one last wave. Arturo had his soldier balanced precariously on a lamp near the playroom's rocking chair, his father already forgotten as he pretended that the soldier was about to leap out of an aircraft. Playing along, Paolo ran to the over-size toy box to dig for something to push the soldier off the lamp.

The nanny was helping him.

Federico shook his head, knowing he'd likely find the lamp broken by the end of the evening. As he closed the door behind him, all desire to attend the dinner vanished. He fervently wished he could dismiss the nanny and spend the evening with his sons himself.

Pia Renati had been one hundred percent right. He spent far more time attending to duty than to his own children.

When he entered the main hallway, Federico's personal assistant fell into step beside him. Without preamble, Teodora began running down the list of events he was to attend over the next few days. Federico only half-listened. He could just imagine Pia's questions if she heard Teodora's description of his upcoming meeting with the leader of the national fishermen's association. Or the speech he planned to deliver at the opening of a new government office building.

Federico wondered if the outspoken, curly-haired blonde could propose a solution to his dilemma as easily as she'd pinpointed it.

He doubted it.

"I'VE BEEN HERE two weeks, and I'm still not convinced you need me," Pia grumbled to Jennifer as she grabbed a bottle of water from a small refrigerator cleverly hidden in an antique armoire. "I swear, there are more people in this place than in the White House and 10 Downing Street combined."

"There are also more people living here, all with royal titles, all of whom work a full schedule. Downside of a big family—it requires more staff, more protection, you name it." Jennifer, whose fiery red hair and soft ivory skin made her look like a beauty queen even at nine months pregnant, let out a not-so-beautiful groan and wiggled her toes.

"But no one to fluff the lady's pillow for her?" Pia teased. "Poor baby."

Jennifer eyed the pillow elevating her feet. "Ha, ha. Even with all the staff in the world, you're still the only person I can gripe to about my swollen ankles. Or about the fact I've been stuck in this room forever. With you, I'm as comfortable as when I'm alone."

"I'm not sure that's a compliment."

Pia screwed the top off the water bottle, then looked up to see

Jennifer giving her a pointed glance. "It *is* a compliment. I don't feel like my privacy's being invaded with you here. I'm hanging out with a friend. And the best part is that you don't slink around the room as if you think I'm some celebrity you can't speak to or look at directly. Joining this family has taken a lot of getting used to."

Jennifer reached forward on the bed to rearrange the pillow so her feet stayed elevated, but gave up when Pia handed her the bottle of water and took over.

Antony had managed a few quick trips home since Pia's arrival, but hadn't been able to stay more than one night at a time. He'd also thanked Pia for staying, telling her it gave him peace of mind to know Jennifer had someone there with whom she could be completely comfortable. Even so, Pia didn't feel like she was doing much. It certainly didn't compare to her usual workload, which kept her on her toes around the clock.

She waved a hand at the fancy linens that covered the bed. "It's nothing like Haffali, is it, Jen? I mean, your nails are done, your hair looks perfect, and swollen ankles or not, you look like a woman suited to wearing a diamond tiara. No one would ever guess you once ran a refugee camp in the middle of a war zone."

Jennifer let out a halfhearted laugh. "No, I guess not. I don't miss the war zone part of it, but I do miss helping people. Stuck in bed like this, I can't even attend charity events. I feel completely useless."

"I think," Pia angled a look at Jennifer's expanding midsection, "you should focus on yourself and your baby right now. Don't get me wrong, we missed your help at camp when you ran off and married a prince, of all people" —she waved a hand at their posh surroundings for emphasis— "but the money you and Antony raised, and the students you sponsored to work at the camp through your scholarship program, helped us relocate the refugees and close the camp months earlier than we could have otherwise. Then you went out of your way to recommend me to World HIV Relief, which has turned out to be a great job. You deserve a break. Enjoy it."

When Jennifer didn't respond, Pia added, "If you absolutely have to do something, brainstorm a way to expand your scholarship program.

You can do that just as well nine months pregnant and lounging in a royal apartment as you did while working in a rusty trailer. Better, even."

Jennifer took a long sip of water, then twirled her finger in the air as if to say, *whoopee*. "Glad to know I can be mistaken for a beached whale and be useful at the same time."

A knock at the door interrupted them, and Pia excused herself to answer it. She greeted the guard, then returned to Jennifer carrying an armload of mail, including at least two dozen handwritten letters and three boxes. "I don't know how you find time for all this," Pia said as she dumped everything on the bed next to Jennifer.

"I usually don't," Jennifer admitted, turning over an envelope to read the engraved return address on the flap. "Harriet handles most of the invitations and routine correspondence. But I'm sick of sitting here and asked her if I could do it to break up my routine."

Pia retrieved a sterling silver letter opener from Jennifer's corner desk, a gift Antony had given his wife shortly after their wedding.

"Looks like I can actually put you to work today." Jennifer peered at the contents of one of the boxes. "I ordered this camera for Antony's birthday, but forgot to have it gift wrapped."

She lifted the camera out of the shipping box to show Pia. "I wanted to give it to him this weekend, since he'll be able to come home for a day before the talks resume, but there's no way I can go all the way to the gift-wrapping room to do it myself. If I give it to one of the staff, they'll spill the beans."

"This place has a gift-wrapping *room*?" Pia set the letter opener on top of the pile of invitations and letters on the bed. "You must be kidding."

Jennifer handed Pia the camera and shrugged. "I know. Outrageous, isn't it? You don't mind doing the wrapping, though, I hope?"

"Of course not. That's why I'm here," Pia replied as she turned the camera over in her hands. Antony would be thrilled with the gift, since he'd be able to use it to shoot photos of his new baby. "I need something to do besides sitting here handing you tissues or getting you water. I don't think I've ever been this lazy in my life."

"I feel the same way," Jennifer admitted. "I keep telling myself it's good for the baby, and that it can't last much longer. Thirty-six weeks down, four to go." She gave Pia directions to the gift-wrapping room, which was located behind the palace's main kitchen, then waved her off.

Pia returned the camera to its shipping box, then strode out of Jennifer and Antony's apartment with the box tucked under her arm. Fresh air from the palace gardens blew in through the open windows lining the hallway, and her steps grew lighter as she breathed in the smell of the freshly cut lawn. Even though wrapping a gift would normally strike her as a mundane task, today it felt liberating.

It had been tough spending much of the two weeks since her arrival sitting still, either reading books in Jennifer's room while her friend napped or bringing Jennifer whatever she needed, so Jennifer was on her feet as little as possible. Jennifer claimed to feel good, and all indications were that her baby was healthy, but the recurrent, unexplained bleeding she'd experienced a few weeks before had concerned the obstetrician enough to urge her not to take any chances. Antony had agreed with the doctor's assessment, despite knowing his wife would be unable to accompany him on local outings, let alone on his trip to the Middle East.

As slothful as Pia felt most days, she knew her presence made Jennifer less lonely, now that Antony was in Israel and difficult to reach. Pia also offered her a safe outlet for discussing her pregnancy and her adjustment to life at La Rocca without fear it would end up as a topic of conversation among the palace staff. Or worse, fodder for the media, should they catch wind of it.

Like Jennifer, Pia was used to moving around, keeping her body as fit as her mind. Reading more than a book a day and watching endless hours of television quickly lost its allure, and Pia found her mind wandering to her job. Once Antony returned home and Jennifer had safely delivered her baby, Pia could move on to her next assignment for World HIV Relief, the Washington, D.C.-based nonprofit group for which she worked. This time she'd be headed for sub-Saharan Africa, where she'd be in charge of the final construction details and staffing of three residences for children who'd lost their parents in the AIDS epidemic. Though the three facilities wouldn't be nearly enough to handle the demand, she took comfort in the thought that at least some orphaned children might find a place to live, fresh food, and a chance at an education. Not to mention the love and comfort the relief workers offered in abundance.

While the centers were under construction, Pia would have the opportunity to travel through Mozambique, South Africa, and Zimbabwe, educating young men and women about the realities of HIV. Hopefully she could prevent them from contracting the virus and leaving behind even more orphans. Though the accommodations wouldn't be nearly as comfortable as what she had now—nothing on earth was as lavish as La Rocca—she relished the chance to help people who needed her. It satisfied her on a soul-deep level to see the difference her efforts made in the life of a poor, needy child or a desperate young woman.

As Pia made her way down the staircase, she reminded herself that her time with Jennifer was a vacation, and that she should try harder to enjoy it. Within a few short weeks she'd probably miss the chance to put her feet up and chat about ordinary things.

At the bottom of the stairs, she took the hallway to her left. Unable to resist her curiosity, she took a quick peek inside the palace library, where Jennifer said several family members kept their personal book collections. There was a serenity to the room, and she'd been told that King Eduardo could occasionally be found in one of its yellow silk chairs late at night, book in hand, when he needed to wind down after a busy day.

Four rooms beyond the library, Pia pushed through the doors leading to the diTalora family's private dining room, which was used for casual meals, as opposed to the state dining room located at the other end of the palace, which was used for state dinners and meals with visiting dignitaries.

Though the bells of San Rimini's largest cathedral, the nearby Duomo, tolled the noon hour loudly enough to be heard inside the palace, the family dining room was unoccupied. Princess Isabella and her new husband, Nick, had just finished a belated honeymoon trip to Fiji, but had stopped in New York on their way home to attend the opening of an exhibit of San Riminian art. Prince Marco and his wife of nearly a year—Jennifer's friend Amanda—were in England on a long-overdue state visit. And King Eduardo rarely enjoyed a meal that wasn't part of one meeting or another.

Pia hadn't expected Federico to be here eating lunch. Really, she hadn't. Still, she was surprised to find herself disappointed at his absence.

She hadn't seen the prince since their brief ride from the airport, but found that he kept entering her thoughts, even when she tried to distract herself with a book or with research for her new assignment in Africa. Pia guessed that with the rest of the family gone and Jennifer eating her meals in her own room, Federico and his sons ate in their apartment.

She lingered for a moment to study the dining room's long table, sideboard, and elegant oil paintings. For most people, such a room would be considered ostentatious. But for the diTalora family, a table near the palace kitchen—whatever the decor of the room—constituted casual dining. They might even show up in polo shirts and slacks here, as opposed to their usual daytime suits.

The refugees she'd worked with would be stunned to enter such a room, let alone dine in it. Pia herself felt the same way as she strode the palace halls and peeked into its sumptuously decorated rooms. It had taken her several days to accustom herself to the beauty of the private palace apartment Jennifer and Antony shared, though Jennifer claimed to have toned it down since marrying Antony and moving in.

Unbidden, an image of what Federico's apartment must look like leaped into her mind. It would be formal, of course. More so than Antony and Jennifer's, given his stiff personality and that of his late wife. Rich fabrics. Children's toys arranged in perfect order. Pricey gifts from foreign dignitaries displayed neatly on the shelves. A huge bed with expensive silk sheets.

Pia shook off that particular image, then wondered if Federico ever felt trapped living in La Rocca. Though Federico grew up in the palace and surrounded by its luxury, before he and Lucrezia married and had children, he'd spent most of his time traveling, representing San Rimini abroad. His life had been filled with adventure—meeting dignitaries, hammering out political and economic agreements, attending endless receptions and charity events. He'd probably seen it all, from countries struggling for survival to superpowers with more economic clout than some continents. He'd spent time in hospital wards talking about needed reforms, met destitute families struggling to make ends meet, and visited well-heeled political leaders who worked behind mahogany desks. As prince, it all came with the job description. It also gave him a wider view of the world.

But now that he was the sole parent to Arturo and Paolo, Federico had severely curtailed the travel surrounding his public duties. It couldn't have been easy for him, spending all his time in one place, just as it hadn't been easy for her over the past two weeks.

But her stay was only temporary. Federico had a permanent adjustment to make.

"Don't think about him," she cautioned herself aloud as she crossed the empty room, her footsteps echoing across the hardwood. She strode through the doors to the tiled palace kitchen, but the image of Federico's high cheekbones and intelligent blue eyes refused to leave her mind.

How could one man, someone she'd only spent half an hour or so talking to, occupy her thoughts to the exclusion of all else?

Boredom. Had to be. Once she was back at work, she'd forget her encounter with Prince Perfect.

After entering the kitchen, one of the cooks steered her toward the door of the palace's old wine cellar, which had apparently been converted into a gift-wrapping center when renovations were made to the kitchen and a new wine cellar constructed. The room still felt like a wine cellar, however, with its Italian tile floors, windowless walls and cool temperature.

A large metal table with enough space to wrap multiple gifts domi-nated the room. Along the far wall, ribbons of various colors hung on oversize spools. To her left and right, where fine wines had once been displayed, wrapping paper appropriate for every imaginable occasion filled racks from floor to ceiling. On either side of the door were clear plastic chests of tape, bows, and gift bags. A paper cutter and several pairs of scissors rested on top of each chest. In a separate organizer, elegant white cards and their accompanying envelopes bore the diTalora family crest, identifying all gifts as coming from the royal family. A number of fountain pens stood in an expensive-looking pen cup nearby.

It put most department store gift-wrapping areas to shame.

Pia set the camera on the metal table and perused the wrapping paper, finally settling on a blue and silver plaid. Festive, yet gentlemanly. She pulled the roll from the wall, placed it on the table, then studied the oversize paper cutter, trying to ascertain the proper way to position the paper in the contraption. Once she figured it out, she loaded the paper onto the spool.

"I believe you have it backward."

Pia jumped, nearly slicing her hand under the blade of the cutter. "Um, Your Highness. I didn't hear you come in."

Federico smiled from the doorway—a polite but reserved smile— then strode to her side, removed the paper from the spool and repositioned it. "If you place it this way, you will get a cleaner cut." He frowned and cocked his head. "Is it correct English to say a 'cleaner' cut?" He repeated the phrase in Italian, to make sure Pia understood his meaning.

"That's correct, Your Highness."

He nodded, as if pleased that he'd come up with the proper phrase, then turned his attention back to the paper cutter. He was about to trim the paper for her, but glanced at the design and stopped short. "Is this for Jennifer?"

"It's a gift for Antony from Jennifer."

"I see. Then you have made a good selection."

He cut the paper to the appropriate size, then slid the sheet across the table to where she'd set the camera.

"I don't mean to be nosy, Your Highness—"

"Please, Ms. Renati. You are a guest of our household and will likely be here for several more weeks. You may feel free to call me Federico."

"All right. Federico." Somehow, it didn't seem appropriate. Not when he still spoke so formally, using phrases like "you may feel free" as if he were granting royal permission, while she had a vocabulary peppered with Americanisms. But she wasn't going to go against his wishes.

Besides, she liked the way his name rolled off her tongue. "Federico" sounded strong, masculine. Ideal for the man standing before her.

"I was wondering what you were doing here," she continued. "I can't imagine you often wander around this part of the palace."

He smiled at that. This time, it was a genuine, I'm-finding-you-entertaining grin that warmed her inside. "No, I do not. But I have a gift for Jennifer." He gestured to the end of the table, and Pia realized he'd set down a book as he'd entered the room. She read the title aloud, unable to keep the surprise out of her voice. *"The Laid-Back Mom's Guide to Baby's First Year?"*

"I purchased it on a trip to the United States a few years ago. I thought Jennifer might appreciate it."

Pia slid him a sideways glance. "Hate to accuse you of lying, but Jennifer wasn't pregnant a few years ago."

He hesitated. "No. So I will tell you a secret."

Pia raised an eyebrow.

"I purchased it for Lucrezia, when she was pregnant with Paolo. But she never found the time to read it. I tried to find a new copy for Jennifer, since I thought it might be to her liking, but it was not available in San Rimini, so...." He held up his palms in a gesture of surrender. "I am afraid you have found me out."

Pia gave the book a pointed look, then grinned at the prince. "In America, that's what's referred to as 'regifting.' People sometimes do it when they receive a gift they don't care for but can't return."

A stunned look passed over Federico's face. "Regifting? And this is common?"

Pia tried—without success—not to crack up at the prince's obvious shock. Regifting wasn't part of the San Riminian vernacular. "Scandalous, isn't it? But don't worry about it. Jennifer's the one who told me about regifting in the first place. She'll be touched by the present, regifted or not."

"You will keep my secret?"

Pia drew a finger across her chest diagonally each way. "Of course."

"Thank you." He turned, surveying the numerous rolls of paper. While he did so, Pia discreetly looked from Federico to the book again. No, she couldn't imagine Lucrezia cracking that spine. But Federico, buying a book on how to be a relaxed mom? That was equally hard to picture. And he'd tried to buy it twice. Apparently there was more to the man than good looks and an aristocratic title.

"Ms. Renati?"

She tore her gaze from the book to find the prince studying her. "Pia. Please."

His eyes warmed. "Pia, then. Would you assist me in selecting wrapping paper? While I am familiar with my brother's taste, I do not know Jennifer's as well as I should."

Pia's nerves settled. "I'd love to." She studied the rolls, finally choosing a simple tone-on-tone blue paper with a scroll and leaf design.

"Should I not use a paper like this?" He fingered a roll with cartoonish pink lambs and blue rabbits on a yellow background.

Pia pulled a face. "Save that for later. This gift is for Jennifer, not the baby. You want something elegant. Pretty."

Federico looked back at the blue paper. "It is fortunate you were here. I would have made a fool of myself."

Pia put her hand on his arm. "No, you wouldn't have. First, because Jennifer isn't judgmental, and second, because most men in your position wouldn't have taken the time to buy such a thoughtful gift, let alone wrap it themselves. I think it's sweet."

Federico's gaze swept low, to where her fingers rested on his arm. She froze, realizing what she'd done. What she was *still* doing.

Making a fool of herself.

CHAPTER 3

FEDERICO OPENED his mouth to speak, hesitated, then gave her a polite smile. "That is kind of you to say."

Pia withdrew her hand from Federico's arm, appalled that she'd put her hand on his arm without thinking. She stepped forward so she couldn't meet his gaze, then took the roll of blue paper off the wall and handed it to him.

Working side by side, she and Federico wrapped their gifts. Except for the rustle of gift wrap being cut and folded, or the occasional sound of tape being torn from its dispenser, the room was silent.

What possessed her? Casually touching a member of the royal family simply wasn't done. Worse, even through the sleeve of his crisp gray shirt, during that brief touch, she'd noticed the corded strength of his forearm and the heat of his body. She'd done it to offer comfort, as she would to any of the hundreds of refugees she'd helped over the years. But this was the first time she'd experienced a physical reaction to such a simple touch, and the thought of it unsettled her.

"It is finished." Federico held up his package. "Would a white bow be appropriate?"

Pia nodded, and Federico turned to select one from the chests near the door while she folded the paper around the end of the camera box.

As she bent to tape down the final flap, something brushed against her elbow. She glanced sideways to see that Federico had sent a large blue bow sliding across the metal table to her.

"I believe Antony would like that one."

She let out a breath, realizing as she did so how nervous his silence made her. "Thank you. It matches perfectly."

She ripped another piece of tape off the dispenser and attached the bow to the box. "See, you do know what you're doing. You didn't need me."

"I beg to differ."

She looked up to retort, but in that moment, she caught a hint of mirth in his eyes that made her wonder if he was flirting. But then Federico pushed open the door to the kitchen, and the sound of morning banter between a cook and a delivery driver broke the spell.

"Shall we take them to Jennifer?" Federico braced the door with his arm, indicating that he expected her to precede him.

"Ah, sure." She grabbed the camera and ducked past him, taking care not to make contact. As they made their way toward Jennifer and Antony's apartment, he described a few of the rooms they passed, their history, and what artifacts they possessed. All the while, Pia tried not to think about how handsome he looked in his gray shirt and charcoal slacks, how clean and wonderful he smelled as he walked beside her, or the rich cadence of his voice as he described his home. The man had charisma. He also made her feel important. They were traits that rarely went hand in hand.

Widower with two kids, she reminded herself as they approached the stairs. *All wrong, no matter his attributes.*

As if summoned by her thoughts, the thumping of small feet and the sound of children's unrestrained laughter carried from some-where above them. Federico frowned to himself, and Pia got the sense that his sons weren't permitted to play in the hallway.

Federico didn't alter his pace, however. Instead, he merely commented, "Those are my sons, Arturo and Paolo. I suspect you will have the opportunity to meet them before they reach their playroom."

"Sounds like they're having a fun day."

"Yes." His voice was calm, but given the grave expression on the prince's face, Pia decided it wouldn't be at all fun to be in the nanny's shoes when Federico reached the top of the stairs.

Just as Pia reached the top step and looked down the hall for the source of the laughter, something flat and brown flashed in her peripheral vision. Immediately, a bolt of pain sliced her temple, nearly knocking her to the ground. As a reflex, she put a hand to her forehead, her fingertips meeting torn skin. She registered a sharp intake of breath coming from across the hall at the same time the rapid pounding of children's feet abruptly stopped.

A hand-carved boomerang lay at her feet. Federico bent to retrieve it, then met her astonished gaze.

"Pia, you are hurt!" He patted his pockets until he located a handkerchief, pressed it to her temple, then herded her toward an antique-looking upholstered chair under one of the hallway's broad windows.

"It's all right," Pia assured him. She'd suffered enough scrapes and tumbles in her line of work to know that no permanent damage was done. No feeling faint, no dizziness. But as she moved to take the handkerchief from Federico and hold it to her head, her hand brushed against his, and she realized that her blood soaked both the cloth and his fingers.

"Who carries a handkerchief anymore?" she asked, hoping to ease Federico's worried look.

"Anyone with my children. You would be surprised how often I find a need for it."

The panicked cry of a child suddenly registered in her mind, and Pia turned to see two young boys cowering against a doorjamb. Though they both had expressive brown eyes very different from Federico's blue ones, their skin tone, facial features and dark hair were identical to the prince's, leaving no doubt as to their heritage.

The younger boy's face fell when she spotted him, his eyes squeezing shut against his tears. Then his mouth dropped open with the heartbroken sadness of a child who realizes that he's unintentionally injured another. The older boy stood behind him, clearly more concerned about his father's reaction than his brother's tears.

However, when Pia caught his eye, the older boy stepped forward. "*Mi dispiace.* I hope it doesn't hurt too much." Then he looked to Federico. In a quieter voice, he said, "I didn't mean to, Papa."

Federico pinned his older son with a look that spoke volumes as to his displeasure. "Arturo, where is Signorina Fennini?"

"I am here, Your Highness." The nanny ran up behind Arturo and Paolo, her breathing ragged, her expression twice as distressed as that of the small boys. "I am terribly sorry, but—"

"Please call my driver. I must take Ms. Renati to the hospital."

Federico must have sensed the protest on Pia's lips, because he turned to her and said, "We have a palace doctor for emergencies, but I believe you will need stitches. It should be done in a hospital, so we can lessen the chance that you will be marked." He frowned before adding, "You understand? *Cicatrice?*"

A scar? Not from a little cut to her forehead. "I don't think you need to—"

"I shall call right now," the nanny interrupted, then turned in the opposite direction.

"Signorina Fennini?"

The nanny turned to face Federico, and Pia's heart sank at his tone. "After you have spoken with my driver, please call my assistant, Teodora. Explain what happened and ask her to arrange for someone else to watch the children tonight."

From the embarrassed look on the nanny's face and the determined one on Federico's, Pia realized she'd just witnessed the nanny being fired. She said nothing, though she felt a wave of sympathy for the young woman.

And then, an overwhelming sense of déjà vu. How old had she been on her own first babysitting job? Not much younger than the nanny. It also ended badly, leaving her with wounds greater than any she had suffered from the boomerang.

Once the nanny left, Pia forced herself to ignore her throbbing head and winked at the boys. "Accidents happen. It's all right." She hoped that Federico got the message as well, and would give the nanny a second chance.

Both boys still looked upset, so Pia used her free arm to make a muscle. "I'm tough. Getting banged in the head is no big deal."

The older boy, Arturo, looked down at his feet, but she could see he hid a smile.

"I'm Pia Renati. What's your name?" Pia asked the younger boy.

"Paolo."

"Paolo. That's one of my favorite names! My father's name was Paolo, and it's my cousin Angelo's middle name."

Arturo raised his head, his face alight. "Viscount Renati? He's a friend of Uncle Antony's."

"He's very nice," Paolo whispered. "He sent Aunt Jennifer pretty flowers after she told us she had a baby growing in her tummy."

Pia grinned, trying to ignore her worsening headache. "That sounds like Angelo."

Beside her, however, Federico grunted.

She didn't spend much time with Angelo, since they possessed such opposite personalities. But given Federico's disapproving reaction, he was apparently familiar with Angelo's reputation for shameless flirting, especially when the press was around to see and photograph him. No wonder Federico suspected that she might not be discreet about Jennifer's condition.

Despite Angelo's public persona, Pia knew he would never give personal information about the royal family to anyone in the media. He respected the diTaloras and valued his friendship with Antony too much. Maybe she could have Jennifer set Federico straight at some point. It would be one less reason for the prince to worry about her.

Which, given the concern etched on his face as he reached over to lift the handkerchief and study her forehead, would be a good thing.

"It's really not that bad, Federico," she assured him as she pressed the handkerchief to her forehead again. "Head wounds tend to bleed a lot. Doesn't mean they're serious."

The prince glanced at his sons. "They should not have been throwing that indoors."

"You were aiming for the window, weren't you, Arturo?" Pia joked. "It *is* open. So that's almost like being outside."

Arturo put a hand over his mouth to hide his grin from his father, and Pia relaxed, knowing the boy was finally at ease. However, Paolo continued to stare at her, wide-eyed. The blood had soaked through the handkerchief to her fingers.

"Paolo, can you do me a favor? Look out the window and see if your father's car is coming."

Paolo moved to the window and stood on tiptoe to get his chin over the level of the sill. "Not yet." He looked over his shoulder and shot her a shy smile. "But I see Nonno. He's coming inside."

Less than a minute later, King Eduardo reached the top of the stairs. He wore a well-tailored navy suit and sky blue shirt that made him appear far younger than his age. His sharp gaze took in the boys, the boomerang, and her bloody forehead. Having sized up the situation, he waved the boys to his side. They moved like lightning, no questions asked.

Pia felt she should stand, but the king waved for her to keep her seat. "Please, there is no need." He shifted his focus to Federico. "I was told downstairs that you're taking her to the hospital?"

"Yes."

Even if she hadn't seen his face on hundreds of newspaper stands or on San Rimini's coins, she'd know Eduardo diTalora to be a king simply by his confident demeanor and the ease with which he directed those around him.

"I am finished with my appointments for today," the king told Federico, "so I shall watch Arturo and Paolo. I can take them to the old armory and show them the weapons and suits of armor Nick has restored. It will be entertaining and they can learn about San Rimini's medieval history."

"Thank you, that would be appreciated." Federico gestured toward a nearby chair, where he'd deposited the wrapped gifts. "Could you also see that these are delivered to Jennifer, and let her know what happened?"

"Of course."

The king had each boy pick up a gift, then he focused on Pia. "Will

Jennifer need assistance while you're at the hospital? I can find someone to stay with her."

Pia shook her head, her temple pounding as she did so. "I think she'd prefer the privacy, Your Highness. I don't imagine I'll be away long."

After offering an apology for his grandsons' antics, and a wish for her speedy recovery, the king ushered the boys down the stairs.

"Thank you for showing such kindness to my sons," Federico said once the king and the young princes were out of earshot. His gaze fixed on her bloodied forehead, but despite the lack of eye contact, his words carried enough emotion to let her know he was truly grateful. "You have a natural ability with children."

She waved it off. "Comes from working with so many of them in refugee camps, I suppose."

Saying a few kind words to a troubled child, whether in a war-torn camp or in a royal palace, didn't translate into natural ability, not compared with what the full-time duty of parenting required, but she wasn't about to contradict the prince. Not when she was holding his handkerchief to her head.

Through the open window, Pia heard the crunch of tires on the gravel drive. Federico glanced out to ensure it was his car approaching, then leaned down, warning her to hold the handkerchief tight against her temple, and lifted her out of the chair and into his arms.

"Your Highness—"

"Federico."

"You...you really don't need to carry me. I'm entirely capable of walking. And I'm getting blood on your shirt."

He tightened his hold. "I have others. Now put your free arm around my shoulders. I do not wish to drop you on the stairs. That would certainly be worse than anything my sons have done to you today."

Pia did as he asked, though he held her securely enough she doubted she would slip. Federico's forehead creased as he carefully made his way down the stairs.

As her palm flattened against his upper back and she felt the expanse of muscle under her arm, Pia closed her eyes, and decided that maybe what his sons had done wasn't so bad.

FEDERICO COULDN'T BELIEVE the knot of press photographers gathered outside the hospital's front door.

He wondered what, exactly, the press had heard: that he was firing his third nanny in two years, that a palace guest had been injured, that his children caused the injury, or worst of all, that he'd been seen carrying a bleeding-but-beautiful blonde from the palace's rear entrance to his private car.

He groaned inwardly. Whichever it was, he'd probably shot his reputation as the grieving widower prince who never made a public misstep in one quick afternoon. Not that he cared. He wouldn't change any of his actions.

He shifted the window blinds for a better look at the photographers and their setup. When he took Pia back to La Rocca, they'd have to use a side or rear exit and hope the media hadn't covered it. If the reporters believed he had a personal connection to Pia, they'd dog her for weeks in anticipation of breaking a story on a royal romance. Not only would that be disturbing to Pia, but their pursuit would likely result in the discovery of Jennifer's prescribed bed rest.

And that would be a *real* story. One with the potential to affect the Middle East talks and millions of lives as a result.

Federico turned away from the window of the small private room where the hospital staff had placed Pia, taking a seat in a well-worn chair to wait while the doctor finished bandaging her temple. As Pia had claimed, the wound wasn't as bad as he'd feared, requiring only three or four stitches.

Federico's level of guilt, however, hadn't lessened. His gut constricted at the knowledge that he'd been responsible.

He snagged a piece of gray fluff from the arm of the chair and flicked it into a nearby garbage can, where it landed on top of the sterile wrapper from Pia's bandage.

Pia had taken the accident in stride, even trying to console the boys. While he appreciated how well she related to them, and how effectively she'd calmed them, he finally understood how his parents had felt when Marco got into a wrestling match with two other boys in kindergarten and the matter became tabloid fodder.

As if he'd failed as a parent.

He'd let his sons get out of control, and someone had been hurt.

The doctor gave Pia instructions for keeping the bandaged area clean, then turned to Federico. "I believe she will heal quickly, Your Highness."

"*Grazie*. I appreciate your prompt attention. Once it's ready, I will settle the bill. I do not wish for Ms. Renati to be responsible."

Pia began to argue, but Federico raised a hand to stop her. "Please. It is the least I can do."

After the doctor nodded and took his leave, Pia shot him an exasperated look. "I am perfectly capable of handling my own medical bills."

"This accident was my fault. Your focus should be on your recovery, not on finances."

She shook her head, making her blond curls bounce. "First of all, there's no recovery to focus on. I'm not an invalid. Second, it wasn't your fault. It could have happened to anyone. Kids do these things."

"Not mine."

She slid off the table where the doctor had attended her. "No offense, but they're children. They have energy. Royal or not, that means they have accidents."

He puffed out a breath. "They do, and I try to be understanding, but unfortunately, the world holds them to a different standard than it does other children. The sooner Arturo and Paolo learn that, the easier it will be for them. It was the same for me, when I was a child."

Without warning, she placed her hand on the back of his, where it rested on the arm of the chair. For a moment, he saw her second-guess herself. But this time—unlike when she'd given him the reassuring touch in the gift-wrapping room, then yanked her fingers away as if she'd touched fire—she decided to leave her hand where it was.

He found he couldn't tear his gaze from those fingers.

When she spoke, her voice barely rose above a whisper. "It must've been difficult, growing up as you did, in the public eye."

"Perhaps." It was the first female contact he'd enjoyed in as long as he could remember without simultaneously fearing the calculation behind it. He met her gaze in an attempt to concentrate on her words instead of her touch. "But I learned to behave and to fulfill my role in the family."

The lesson hadn't ended in childhood. It continued with his marriage to Lucrezia and in the way he raised his children. It affected the way he related to anyone and everyone whose life crossed paths with his.

He forced himself to project composure, despite the feel of Pia's fingertips slipping across his knuckles, drawing away his frustration. He could grow used to her soft touch. He'd even enjoyed carrying her to his waiting car, and had regretted that an orderly had met them at the hospital so he couldn't carry her inside.

Which meant he'd enjoyed it too much.

Unfortunately, Pia's pure-hearted gesture made him all the more susceptible to her other charms: her freckle-faced blond beauty, her unassuming attitude, her warm smile. For a brief moment, he had the urge to pull her close and kiss her. Would she brush him aside? Or return it?

He thought—maybe—she'd return it, but he drove back the impulse. It wasn't wise to think about Pia Renati, not in that way. No matter how much he enjoyed talking with her, no matter how she treated his sons or how attractive he found her, he couldn't handle the public response to his having a romantic life. *Any* romantic life. Nor could he handle it personally. He'd confused friendship and comfort with love once before and swore never to do it again.

She hesitated for a moment, as if sensing the turmoil within him. She withdrew her hand but maintained eye contact. "I hope you'll forgive me for saying so, because I know it's not my place, but you shouldn't be upset with the nanny. I would hate to see her fired because I didn't duck in time."

A nurse walked by, slowing her pace to peek in the door as she passed. Realizing their private room probably wasn't so private, Federico stood and gestured for Pia to accompany him.

Once they were in the hall leading out of the emergency wing, he picked up their earlier conversation, but was careful to keep his voice low. "Please do not concern yourself over the nanny. You cannot be expected to dodge boomerangs while walking through the palace. And unfortunately, this was not the first incident. My concerns with the nanny go beyond today."

He wanted to say more, but they had arrived at the nurses' station, where Federico had promised the doctor he'd stop to speak with the staff and shake hands. For the first time in memory, he had no wish to engage in routine socializing, an act that was second nature to him.

He wanted to talk to Pia, to convince her that he'd given the nanny every opportunity, and that he tried to be tolerant of his children and their rambunctious play. Most of all, he wanted Pia to see how much he loved his sons.

He'd lay down his life for Arturo and Paolo without hesitation.

A quarter hour later, Pia completed her paperwork and Federico's driver approached the nurses' station to let him know he was parked at the rear of the hospital.

"I fear we will not make as quiet an exit as we did an entrance." The driver, who'd been with the family since Federico was a boy, led them down an isolated staff-only hallway to avoid the gauntlet of the public areas. "There are reporters at every door, even the rear."

Federico considered the situation. "In that case, bring the car to the west entrance. If we cannot escape them, we may as well face them and answer their questions. Make it clear there's nothing scandalous happening. But I would like you nearby, with the car running, so we can leave as soon as possible."

The driver gave a businesslike nod, then walked ahead of them to retrieve the car.

"I don't need to talk to anyone, do I?" Pia asked once the driver was out of earshot. "I wouldn't have the foggiest notion what to say. And I'm a total mess."

"They will most likely focus on me. If you stand back, they should leave you alone." He smiled and hoped it was reassuring.

"Well, that's good." A nervous edge crept into her voice as she added, "I wish I had a mirror. I'm sure my mascara has smeared, and—"

"Stop." He reached out and spun her to face him. The fluorescent lights of the staff hallway cast her skin in a less-than-flattering shade of yellow, but that wouldn't affect her outside. And he wasn't sure how her hair was supposed to look, but the tangle of curls seemed no more out of place than usual. He pulled a stray piece of white lint from the front of her blouse, then tucked a loose curl behind her ear. "Your mascara looks fine. Do you have any lipstick?"

"Nope. No purse, no lipstick." She took a deep breath, then grinned, "I look washed out, don't I?"

It took him a beat to grasp the phrase *washed out*, then he shook his head. "No, not at all. My sister always says that good lipstick is her savior when her hair or clothing choice feels less than perfect. I thought it would take the attention away from the bandage on your forehead."

"Is it that bad?"

"No. In fact, you look quite good for a woman who has just had stitches." And he meant it. Most people would have crumbled—at least to some extent—when struck by a boomerang, let alone when sitting through a stitching session, then being told afterward that they'd face dozens of reporters. But Pia possessed an inner strength he admired. He'd bet that boomerang that she'd never been one for drama. She was too upbeat and assured.

And she was unlike any of the over-perfumed, painstakingly styled women who frequented palace functions, and who primarily spoke to him in hopes he would move them ahead socially or financially.

"That's not saying a lot."

"You'll be fine."

He reached to free a few strands of hair that were trapped under the edge of the white gauze.

Pia's breath caressed the inside of his wrist as she spoke. "All right. Nothing I can do at this point anyway, so I'll take your word for it."

"Good."

Her fingers went to the front of his shirt. "You still have blood all over your shoulder."

"I told you, I have other shirts. Perhaps it will not show on camera."

"It'll definitely show."

"It does not matter."

He lowered his hand to her shoulder, then bent to drop a soft kiss near her bandage. He intended it to be a quick peck, a confidence boost before she faced the cameras outside. But then his lips lingered against her soft skin, and his eyes closed as he savored the forbidden sensation of her curls brushing his face.

Oh, he was fooling himself. He had no intention of making this quick.

He heard the stutter in her breathing, felt her fingertips feather against his chest where she'd bloodied his shirt. In that moment, his carefully scheduled, precisely planned world came undone.

CHAPTER 4

THIS WAS what it was like to act on lust, to allow his body and his desires to rule the moment.

A soft sound escaped Pia's lips as their mouths met and they shared a long, slow kiss. Federico forced himself to breathe, to hold back from the warmth and comfort and passion he knew she possessed, despite the fact that every ounce of his being ached for it.

But even keeping their kiss on the gentle end of the scale, he recognized the danger. Kissing Pia—a commoner who didn't automatically extend her hand so he'd help her into a car, who protested when he carried her, who likely preferred sweatpants to skirts and spoke to his children as if she understood their impulses—meant surrendering to every temptation he'd been taught to avoid since childhood.

Yet here he was, in one of the few moments of his life not taking place before cameras or dignitaries—or under his father's watchful eye—and damn if he wasn't considering what might be.

He broke the kiss, reluctantly, unwilling to keep his mouth more than a whisper away from hers. He used both hands to ease her curls away from her face, and saw her eyes fill with a longing that likely mirrored his own.

As much as he wanted her, as much as his body ached to give her a full-blown, earth-shattering kiss, to see where it might lead and whether it would quench his desire, he couldn't do it.

He was overwhelmed by how badly he wanted to kiss her, to taste her, to feel her body molded against his, especially when he knew what could happen the moment they stepped outside this hallway. He couldn't handle the risk of the press seeing him as anything other than Prince Perfect, the man who lived up to their lofty ideals. In the long run, it would hurt his family and his country. It would also hurt Pia.

Leading her on—kissing her again—would be wrong.

"Pia," the sound of his voice cut through the silence of the empty hallway. "I—"

He lost his train of thought as her fingers toyed with a button on the front of his shirt.

"You what?" She looked up. Her gaze locked with his, and a connection he'd never had with another human being sizzled between them.

All thought of ideals fled his mind as he closed his eyes and kissed her again, succumbing to her touch, her look. He trapped her body against the cinder block hospital wall, reveled in the sensation of her firm breasts pressed to his chest, her warm mouth pressed to his.

She opened to him, her tongue tasting and teasing his. Then her hands dropped from his chest and snaked around his waist, pulling him tighter against her. But there was still an innocence about her, a quality to her kisses that told him this wasn't a common occurrence for her, either, and that she'd sensed the same unique connection between them that he had.

If he wasn't a prince, he'd be tempted to pull her into a side room and make love to her right then and there. To act as anyone else would do. He'd never felt such an emotional bond with Lucrezia, or such an overwhelming physical need.

Damn.

He pulled back from Pia once more, his body giving an involuntary shudder at the unwanted separation.

Two years had passed since Lucrezia's death. In the public's mind

—and sometimes even in his own—it was like yesterday. Only last week he'd attended the opening of a school library that had been named for her, built with funds she'd raised through her charitable work. Nothing having anything to do with intimacy should be entering his mind. No matter how powerful the connection, no matter what the circumstances. What kind of person was he, kissing a woman when his wife had been dead and buried such a short time and he had two young sons?

"I am sorry, Pia," he managed. "This...this is not appropriate."

"I understand." Her hands dropped from his waist. "I shouldn't have assumed—"

"No. It is nothing you have done. If I were any other man, I would not hesitate to—" His gut twisted. He didn't remember the last time he didn't have the right words for an occasion, or the last time he'd suffered such abject embarrassment. He sighed and smoothed his hand over her hair again. "I would not hesitate. I find you fascinating. But my life is not my own. I have obligations to my family and my country. People have certain expectations of me as a prince."

"And with Lucrezia?"

"It is not that." He exhaled in a huff. How could he say this so Pia would understand, when he hardly understood it himself? He wanted to kiss her, desperately. But another part of him felt it went against rules he was bound to follow, particularly in honoring Lucrezia's memory. "Though to some extent, I suppose it is."

"You don't need to explain. It's okay," Pia straightened and gave him a smile, but her words tumbled over one another in her haste to get them out, belying her nervousness. "We should leave, anyway. Your driver must have the car ready by now, and the reporters will wonder where you are."

He swallowed, wanting to say something more, to settle things between them, but all his years of etiquette lessons and experience in diplomacy failed him. He simply turned and began walking toward the double doors at the end of the hallway that led to the hospital's west entrance. Pia walked at his elbow. Just before they reached the doors, a laugh escaped her. He stopped and stared at her, incredulous.

"You are amused?"

"Well, at least I shouldn't need lipstick anymore."

"No, I suppose not." His mouth spread into a slow smile at her attempt to defuse the tension simmering between them. He liked her more and more each time she spoke. However, when he looked ahead, through the door's square, eye-level window to see what lay beyond, he found himself working to keep the smile on his face.

At least thirty reporters and their camera crews jammed the area outside the hospital's revolving door. Behind the tangle of people stood two rows of news vans, most topped with blinding lights and satellite dishes. It was almost as bad as it had been when he and Lucrezia left the hospital following the births of their sons.

"Here goes nothing," whispered Pia, her voice serious as she surveyed the scene beyond the doors.

"It will be nothing," Federico assured her. "I speak with the press several times a week. You need only stand beside me. My driver knows to make a subtle interruption and escort us to the car if anything goes amiss. But it will not."

The reporters caught sight of the pair as they pushed out of the hallway and into the lobby, then through the glass revolving doors at the hospital's main entrance. Immediately, the reporters elbowed forward, knocking into hospital security as they began vying for the prince's attention.

"Your Highness!"

"How is Pia Renati?"

"Can you tell us why Pia Renati is at the palace?"

"Tell us why you're at the hospital today, Prince Federico!"

At the cacophony of rapid-fire Italian, Pia stiffened beside him. He put a hand to the small of her back and eased her forward at the same time he waved for the crowd to quiet down and take a step back.

Once the throng receded and Pia was no longer in danger of being jostled, he removed his hand from her back and folded both hands in front of him, as if he were about to speak at a formal event. Keeping his voice well-modulated, he began, "Thank you for your concern. Judging from your presence, you have heard that a palace guest suffered a minor injury today. She has seen a doctor and all is well. I'm happy to answer your questions, but I have only a moment. As you might imagine, she needs her rest. I also believe that, as a private citizen, it's important that all of us respect her privacy."

A familiar reporter from one of San Rimini's local news stations thrust a microphone forward. "Your Highness, can you tell us what happened this afternoon, and about the purpose of Pia Renati's visit to the royal palace?"

"Good evening, Amalia," he greeted her in the light, practiced tone he always used with members of the press. "Ms. Renati is a friend of the family. She was playing with my sons this afternoon and suffered a cut to her temple. Thankfully, she has been treated and is on the mend." He shot the lean brunette reporter a grin and added, "Nothing more serious than when you had the dog loose in your studio last week."

Amalia nodded her thanks, smiling over the memory of the dog being showcased on their animal adoption segment that had escaped its leash in the middle of the broadcast, knocking the evening news anchor out of his chair. Happy to have her sound bite, she nodded to her cameraman that they should depart for their next assignment.

Another reporter stepped forward, one Federico recognized from the tabloid newspaper *Today's Royals*. Federico gave the woman a welcoming smile, but steeled himself for what would undoubtedly be a personal question.

"Your Highness" —the reporter jabbed her phone over the shoulder of a hospital security guard so it was nearer Federico's face— "isn't it true that Pia Renati has been staying at the palace for more than two weeks? Certainly that constitutes something more than a friend of the family. Care to comment?"

A rumble went through the reporters and they started shouting questions again. Federico raised his hand for quiet while he wracked his brain for a suitable yet vague answer, but the crowd only grew louder. The reporter from *Today's Royals* continued to ignore the hospital security guard, who asked her to take a step back, but worse than that, her question had caught the attention of all the other reporters. Even Amalia had perked up and directed her cameraman to turn around and get a close-up of Federico's reaction.

"We understand your nanny, Mona Fennini, was dismissed today, though she has been on staff for only a few months," the reporter raised her voice, making sure the crowd heard her clearly. "And you now say that Pia Renati was playing with your sons this afternoon. Is she being considered for the position of nanny?"

"As I said, Pia Renati is a friend of the family. We often have close friends stay for extended periods, especially when they've traveled from a distance."

Federico turned to another reporter, but the woman from *Today's Royals* wasn't satisfied. In a voice loud enough for all the others to hear, she asked, "Is there a relationship between you and Pia Renati the press should know about? A reason she was playing with your sons?"

Federico ignored the reporter and asked the others if they had further questions. At the same time, he slid a glance toward his driver, who recognized the signal and eased the Mercedes forward, scattering the reporters at the rear of the pack.

"Your Highness, does Pia Renati's presence at the palace have something to do with Jennifer?" A man he recognized from an Italian network waved his hand so Federico would see that he was the one who asked the question. "My sources indicate that Pia used to work for Jennifer at the Haffali refugee camp. Prince Antony's wife has not been seen in public in several weeks, and it's rumored that she's experiencing difficulty with her pregnancy."

"She did not accompany Prince Antony to Israel, as originally planned," added another voice from somewhere in the crowd. It sounded like a reporter he knew from *San Rimini Today*. "Care to comment on that?"

Anxious to cut off any questions about Jennifer— and the state of her pregnancy—Federico shook his head. His voice adamant, he answered, "As you know, the meeting in Israel began over a month later than originally intended. My sister-in-law is now beginning her ninth month of pregnancy. Therefore she is keeping to a limited schedule and, as is true of most women approaching a due date, she is no longer traveling out of the country."

"Is that all?" the *Today's Royals* reporter pressed. "She had been making public appearances locally until shortly before Ms. Renati arrived in country. But on the day before Ms. Renati's arrival, she canceled a fundraising dinner at the French embassy for her scholarship project with almost no notice. Are there pregnancy complications? Is that why Ms. Renati is here?"

"I'm afraid you've made several incorrect assumptions," Pia's voice startled him. He'd encouraged her to speak English to him, giving him some practice at the language from formal events, so he'd never heard her smooth, San Riminian-accented Italian. "As His Highness has stated—"

"Isn't it unusual in your line of work to have so much time off? Or are you no longer employed by World HIV Relief?" the reporter persisted, pushing her phone toward Pia's nose this time. "It seems like quite a coincidence."

Federico saw her expression shift as she scrambled for an answer. He turned to address the reporter, to rescue her, but Pia spoke first. "I've just wrapped up a project in the United States and have not yet moved on to my next assignment. It was the perfect time to visit a dear friend."

"You're in between assignments?" The reporter's eyes brightened. "So you are technically unemployed for the moment. Does that mean you're considering a position in the palace?"

"As a nanny to Prince Arturo and Prince Paolo, perhaps?" Amalia added, winking at Federico as if she'd caught on to a palace secret.

"If you did enough research to know that I'm employed by World HIV Relief, then you know I'm just that…employed. Quite happily."

At that moment, Federico's driver came around the side of the Mercedes and opened the door. Federico raised a hand to the reporters. "I apologize for cutting this short, but I am due back at the palace for a function. And I am sure Ms. Renati could use time to rest. What happened today was an accident, but a minor one involving a palace guest. That's the entire story. If you need anything more, you are welcome to contact my office to schedule a separate interview."

He thanked the group, waving and smiling as he moved to the car. He waited for Pia to enter, then strode around to the opposite side and slid into the seat. Once the doors were closed, he signaled the driver to head back to La Rocca.

"I was trying to help. Sorry if I said the wrong thing," Pia spoke in English again, turning in her seat to glance back at the scattering reporters behind them. "I thought saying I was between assignments would get them off the topic of Jennifer. I promised Jennifer...I didn't think...well, it didn't occur to me they'd believe I'm your children's nanny. I'm supposed to start work in Africa shortly. If they'd done their research, they'd know that."

"It is quite likely they do know, but hoped to obtain more information by pretending ignorance." Even as he answered, his mind was focused on her earlier words, which sparked an idea. She had been good with the boys. And he knew from palace gossip that she had little to do, besides keep Jennifer company.

He ventured, "The boys took to you this afternoon. Surprisingly so, as they are usually tentative around strangers. They begin school again the day after tomorrow and will only be home a few hours in the afternoons. If you were interested—"

"You have got to be kidding." Her eyes widened, then she added, "I'm sorry. That came out wrong. Your boys really are sweet. But Jennifer needs me."

She looked down as she said the last part, though, and he couldn't help but tease her. "But you are bored, yes?"

"I never said that."

He pinned her with a look, and she raised a hand over her head to wave an imaginary white flag. "Fine. You've caught me. I'm bored senseless. It's not that I don't enjoy spending time with Jennifer. I do. She's a dear friend. But there isn't much for me to do. The pregnancy is tiring to her at this point, and she's not sleeping well at night—not that anyone could with a watermelon-size baby making it impossible to get comfortable—so she naps a lot during the day."

"Then you might consider—"

"No. Don't even think it. I would be the worst nanny in the world. Besides, I have a job. As I said, I'm due to travel to Africa in a few weeks. Once I'm there, I'll be incredibly busy, so a little boredom is probably good for me right now."

An odd note had crept into her voice, and he could tell she was fighting to temper it. Was it because she objected to being a nanny, he wondered, or *his* nanny? After what had happened between them in the hospital hallway, it made sense.

But he'd never seen anyone able to put Paolo and Arturo at ease so quickly. With her years of experience as a relief worker, no doubt she possessed solid organizational skills. She wouldn't lose Arturo in the palace gardens or spend hours on the phone talking fashion and boys with her friends, as Mona had.

He shrugged, though the more he thought about it, the more the idea appealed to him. "It will be several weeks before I can find a full-time nanny," he explained, forcing himself to sound casual. "I only thought that, given how easily you related to my sons this afternoon, you might want to spend an hour or two a day with them until it is time for you to leave. Just to ease your boredom."

She started to shake her head, but he cut her off by adding, "It would distract the reporters from Jennifer's pregnancy. I did not think they would focus on her health as much as they did. Their suspicions will only worsen until the baby is born."

"I don't know."

"I would not consider you an employee. You are a family friend, and—"

And *more.* That was the problem. If he were honest with himself, he was asking her because he wanted to spend time with her, learn more about her. He'd only seen her once since she'd arrived at the palace, and the reporters' pestering questions gave him the perfect excuse. In a few weeks, she'd be gone. Even if he could never touch her again, enjoying her company and easy conversation brought him back to life, both in mind and body.

And, if only for his boys, he needed to feel alive again. Feel an emotion, any emotion. Something to jerk him out of the passive life he'd been living. Perhaps then he could renew his excitement in his position and responsibilities.

"And?"

Her soft voice pulled him out of his thoughts. He shrugged, hoping he appeared nonchalant. "And I hope you will think about it. Next time Jennifer is taking a nap, feel free to come to my apartment and see the children."

He intentionally left out *and me*.

"Your Highness, we are here."

Federico blinked at the driver's words, startled to see that they'd passed through the palace gates and were rolling through the gardens that abutted the rear entrance.

"Would you like me to assist you to Antony and Jennifer's apartment?" Federico hated for their time together to end. He still wanted to apologize for what had occurred in the hospital, and at the same time, he desperately wanted it to happen again.

"I'll be fine. Thanks." Her color was high as she spoke, and he knew her mind was on the hospital hallway, too.

Pia let herself out of the car before the driver had exited the vehicle, smiled over her shoulder, and scurried up the stairs and out of sight.

Federico thanked his driver, then slowly ascended the stairs.

"Idiot, idiot, idiot!" Pia grumbled under her breath as she hurried through an empty palace hall toward Jennifer's apartment. What was she thinking, kissing Prince Perfect? Or worse, making it so clear she enjoyed it?

He might have started it, but after he pulled away, obviously realizing he'd touched his lips to those of an idiot who didn't belong in his circle, she kept playing with his shirt button and looking up at him like some lovesick groupie. A man with two kids. A man whose activities were public knowledge to half the western world. A man totally beyond someone like her, *if* she even wanted a romantic relationship, which she didn't.

But holy romantic royalty, what a kiss.

She tried to appear composed when she passed a guard walking through the hallway leading to Jennifer and Antony's private apartment, but as soon as she rounded the corner and was out of his sight, she ran a hand over her hair, remembering how he'd smoothed it back from her face.

Federico's embrace felt as amazing as she'd imagined when she'd sat beside him in the back of the Mercedes on the way to La Rocca from the airport. His kiss, however, demonstrated far, far more passion than she would have guessed the ever-appropriate Prince Federico possessed.

What was his real story? Pia wondered. And how much emotion bubbled under his stoic facade? Because after seeing the concern etched on his face while the doctor gave her stitches, and witnessing the regret in his eyes when she'd mentioned the nanny, Pia knew that he was a more complex man than the media, and perhaps even Federico himself, believed. He'd meant that kiss, body and soul. No one who still truly mourned a beloved wife could kiss like that. It wasn't possible. Even his words made it clear. He'd pulled back from the kiss because of society's dictates—not because of what he felt in his own heart.

If Federico was half as transfixed by her as she was by him, then he was hurting, because the connection she felt was seismic.

Pia let out a long, cleansing breath as she keyed in the code to enter Jennifer's apartment, and told herself not to think about it. Nothing would come of it, so why get her stomach in knots?

"Fine. Don't think about it," Jennifer retorted, causing Pia to jump. "But you have to know that I absolutely hate you right now."

Pia stopped just inside the door to Jennifer's sitting room and stared at her friend, unsure what she could possibly have done to make Jennifer upset. And aggravated with herself for talking out loud, again. At least she hadn't mentioned Federico's name while she'd been muttering to herself.

Had Jennifer already seen the evening news? They couldn't possibly have reported her hospital visit so quickly, or the fact that Jennifer's pregnancy might be at risk.

Pia raised a quizzical eyebrow at the redhead, who sat sideways on the sofa, her feet propped on pillows. "You hate me?"

Jennifer swept a hand to encompass her body from shoulders to feet. "Here I am, a contender for the title of Largest Pregnant Woman Ever, and you're standing beside Federico on my TV screen without looking the requisite ten pounds heavier. And after getting hit in the head! I hate you."

Pia rolled her eyes and grinned. She should have known Jennifer was teasing. But after today's emotional ups and downs, anything was possible.

"They already broadcast it?"

"They did." Jennifer clicked off the television, which she'd had on mute, before tossing the remote to an empty spot near her feet. "Five o'clock news. Most of the local channels opened their broadcast right at the hospital, saying," she dropped her voice to a television announcer's tone, "Prince Federico diTalora and Pia Renati, a palace guest, left the hospital only moments ago."

Pia let out a deep sigh. "Well, quit hating me. The last thing I wanted to do today was end up on television. I made a complete fool of myself."

Jennifer's face immediately turned sympathetic. "First, you did not make a fool of yourself. And second, I owe you an apology. What happened is really my fault. I should have thought about the media before I invited you here. At some point, reporters poke into everything this family does. And everything our friends do, too, unfortunately."

"It's fine."

"I wouldn't call it fine," Jennifer argued. "In any case, I really appreciate that you stuck up for me. I had no idea that the press was already speculating about my pregnancy."

"Don't worry about it. I suspect they were fishing for a story. No one expects you to be out and about this close to your due date. But next time, you'll have to wrap your own gift. I'm no good at dodging boomerangs."

Jennifer directed her gaze toward Pia's forehead and winced. "Does it hurt?"

"Not really. I've had much worse."

"I'm sure the boys are upset about it. They're great kids. They just have a lot of energy."

"It was an accident. I just...oh, boy, Jen." Pia sank down on the chair adjacent to the sofa. "I didn't mean to get their nanny fired. I feel horrible."

Horrible was only the beginning. When Federico had given the nanny that look in the palace hallway, right before he'd told the young woman to make other arrangements for the children's care for the rest of the day, Pia had been overwhelmed by her own memories.

At sixteen, she'd lost her one—and only—babysitting job. It was her sole means to earn money and exercise some independence, to prove to herself and her mother that she could manage a job taking care of children. And she'd blown it, big time. The five-year-old girl trusted to her care had fallen off a swing when Pia had pushed her too high, landing hard on her back and shoulders. Those terrifying seconds when Pia saw the young girl tumbling backward out of her seat, with her long brown braid flying over her head and her screams ripping through the air of the peaceful backyard were forever imprinted on Pia's memory. Thinking about it still brought back the horrid nausea Pia had experienced in that moment. Then there was the disgusted glare the child's father had given her when he'd arrived home to see Pia fighting back tears as the paramedics loaded his daughter into the back of the ambulance. That look had shredded her.

"Please," Jennifer nailed Pia with a chastising look. "You were not the cause of the nanny getting fired today. That's the third time in the past month Mona lost track of Arturo and Paolo. One time, Paolo wandered off and was found hiding behind a planter near the state dining room, which is at the opposite end of the palace from Federico's apartment. It's one thing for a nanny to let kids run around in a regular house. It's another in a royal palace where state business is being conducted. Apparently she was on her phone, sending messages back and forth with her friends, and didn't realize Paolo was gone for nearly an hour. She was bound to get fired."

"It must be hard on the boys, though." Pia knew well enough from her own childhood, when her mother shuffled her from house to house. She hated being cared for by her mother's friends while her mother attended parties at all hours, sometimes far from home. Of course, Sabrina Renati had been required to attend those parties, as a professional event planner, but it hadn't made the situation easier for Pia.

All Pia ever wanted during her childhood was a place of her own to run and play, and to have one person who paid attention and took care of her.

"Losing their mother, and now a third nanny, in less than two years? That's awful." Pia added.

"It is, and we do our best to give them stability, all of us. Nick and Isabella read stories to the boys every single night. It's a ritual they've all come to enjoy. Before I got stuck on bed rest, I was teaching them how to play checkers. And Marco has them all excited about a two-week learn-to-ski program in Austria he plans to register them for this winter." She let out a tired breath. "We're trying hard. Federico's had a rotten run of luck with nannies. But the boys know they're loved, by their father most of all."

Pia nodded her understanding at the same time she gestured to the television. "You mind turning it on again? The six o'clock news will be on soon, and I want to see how bad the press made me sound."

"Go right ahead."

Pia retrieved the remote control and clicked on the television. She took a measure of comfort in the fact that so many people cared about Arturo and Paolo, but a slew of aunts and uncles—or friends of the family—didn't make up for the fact they'd lost their mother. Especially when their father's job required such long hours.

"You know, the reporters actually had a good idea," Jennifer commented as the dramatic music opening San Rimini's evening news began to play and computer-generated graphics flashed across the television screen.

Pia dropped into her chair again, then angled it for a better view of the television. "How so?"

"About you being Paolo and Arturo's nanny."

Was this a conspiracy? A bona fide snort escaped Pia. "Maybe I can apply to be King Eduardo's personal assistant while I'm at it. Or, hey, how about Marco's valet? He usually looks like he could use someone to iron his clothes. Just how many jobs are open at the palace? I can get my résumé together and—"

"I'm being serious," Jennifer countered, raising a pillow and pretending to throw it in Pia's direction. "You nearly exploded with joy when I asked you to wrap a present, just so you'd have something to do besides fetch me drinks or blankets or sit in the corner reading your umpteenth book."

"Didn't I tell you to wrap your own presents from now on?"

Jennifer ignored the comment, barreling ahead. "I think you'd be a great nanny. Well, not a nanny, per se. But while I'm napping or otherwise taken care of, it might be fun to spend some time with the boys. They'd love it, and it would give you a chance to get outdoors and enjoy the sunshine." She rubbed her hands together, forging ahead despite Pia's protests. "If you took them to the Palazzo d'Avorio, you could get some beach time with total privacy. Only the royal family uses it, and it's right on the water. I'm sure Federico wouldn't mind."

"No way. I'm the last person in the world who should be taking care of kids," Pia argued, keeping one eye on the screen as the weatherman pointed out current temperatures on his map of southern Europe. Early September was a fabulous time to enjoy San Rimini's beaches, but not as Jennifer suggested.

"You took care of plenty when we worked together at Haffali."

"No, I didn't. Most of them had at least one parent in the camp. I made them balloons out of surgical gloves or taught them how to do cat's cradle. That's different than being someone's full-time parent. Or even a babysitter. I wasn't responsible for them."

"I don't see how playing with Federico's kids is any different than what you did at Haffali." Jennifer argued, her own thoughts obviously returning to the refugee camp where they'd both worked. "You're right, of course, that Paolo and Arturo have every luxury while the kids we cared for were running from a war. But the concept is the same. Kids like to have someone spend time with them. And you're responsible. I've seen it up close and personal, under stressful circumstances, and I saw how much you enjoyed it. I remember you laughing yourself silly one afternoon playing cards with a group of boys in the children's ward." Jennifer hesitated. "Unless there's some other reason you don't want to be around Arturo and Paolo. Or Federico."

Boom.

Pia kept her eyes glued to the broadcast, unwilling to meet Jennifer's gaze. Jen would know in a second that something had happened between her and Federico. She had a knack for reading people's emotions, her friends' most of all. It was part of the reason Antony fell in love with her, part of what made her so well loved by the people of San Rimini.

But Pia wasn't about to admit to her attraction to Federico, not even to Jennifer. Or the twinge in her gut that made her wonder if she actually *could* handle Arturo and Paolo for an afternoon or two.

For all their rambunctiousness, the boys' sweet faces had touched her heart. And, as Jen pointed out, it would get her outside, enjoying fresh air and exercise.

She remained riveted on the news, even though the coverage switched to a traffic report. She shouldn't take the boys by herself, she reasoned. She'd need another adult along, for her own peace of mind if nothing else, and that meant time with Federico.

But perhaps, if she spent more time around the prince, she'd realize how absurd her attraction was. Any thoughts of having a romantic relationship with him were…well, she may as well ask last year's Academy Award Best Actor winner out on a date.

Pia shifted in the chair to face her friend. By the time she was scheduled to leave for Africa, she'd have Federico out of her system. No problem.

"I suppose, if it'll keep the press from asking more questions about you, and if I'm not solely responsible for them, *and* if you don't need me, I'll spend some time with the kids."

Jennifer's mouth spread into a broad, knowing grin. "Perfect."

CHAPTER 5

"I'VE RECONSIDERED YOUR OFFER."

Federico looked up from his copy of *San Rimini Today* to see Pia standing at the entrance to his family's private dining room. Her feet remained on the hallway side of the threshold, her fingers hooked tentatively around the frame of the door, but her I-hope-I'm-welcome smile made his morning.

He wondered how long she'd been standing there, debating whether to enter. It was fairly early, but he sensed she'd been awake for some time. Her clothes appeared fresh and unwrinkled, and her hair tidier than usual. The large gauze bandage she'd worn while leaving the hospital had been replaced by one just large enough to cover the stitches.

She was not, however, wearing lipstick.

He gestured to the large trays laden with eggs, bacon, toast, and fresh fruit that covered the table, trying to distract himself from the type of hunger thoughts of the hospital hallway—and her delicious, unlipsticked mouth—conjured.

"Please, join me. It was only put out a moment ago, and the kitchen staff prepares enough to feed the whole family, even when I dine alone."

Pia hesitated for a moment, then crossed the room and slid into a chair directly across from Federico. "Thank you. I get so used to eating whatever comes out of a can while I'm on assignment, I forget what real food tastes like until I return to the States, or come here to San Rimini." Her eyes widened as she surveyed her choices. "This is what I miss most when I'm working in a remote location. Not television or reliable Internet. Not even air conditioning. I miss hot, fresh food."

He couldn't help but grin. "As you can see, I am quite spoiled. Though I admire you for your work in less than favorable conditions."

She said nothing, but he could tell his comment pleased her. He urged her to help herself, then watched while she poured herself a cup of coffee and added a splash of milk, skipping the cream and the sugar. The same as he took it. As she raised the cup to her lips, he wondered what other quirks they might have in common.

He tore his gaze from her lips and directed a look toward her forehead. "How is your injury? I hope you are feeling better today."

She nodded, the muscles in her face visibly relaxing after she had a sip of the hot liquid. "Fine."

He tried to mask the edginess she triggered in him by neatly folding the paper, careful to keep the headline out of her view, then placing it to the side of his plate. He wondered if he owed her surprise dining room visit to the morning edition, which included a front-page story claiming that—in their words—bizarre events occurred behind the scenes at the palace this week, and speculating about Pia's involvement.

"So," he said. "You wish to reconsider my offer?"

"To visit with the kids," she clarified. She glanced at him over the rim of her coffee cup. "Play with them after school, keep them company, that sort of thing. At least until you find a regular nanny. Jennifer suggested I take them to the Palazzo d'Avorio, get a little sun and beach time for them and for myself while she's napping. If they're even interested. They probably aren't."

He forced himself not to smile at her disclaimers. "On the contrary, I think they would like that very much." He started to pick up the paper out of habit, then thought better of it. Clearly, Pia was nothing like her cousin Angelo, who would have entered the room waving a headline that discussed his private life as if he'd won a prize. If she hadn't mentioned it by now, she probably hadn't even seen the headline, so why stir the eddies of sexual awareness skittering between them into outright turbulence? If anything, he needed to clear the air. He took a deep breath before plunging in. "Pia, about yesterday—"

"It's okay," she waved him off. "We don't need to talk about it."

"But should we not—"

"It was unavoidable. No need to discuss it, since it's not likely to happen again."

He opened his mouth, then closed it. Was she talking about the kiss, as he was? Or the boomerang?

Maybe she'd seen the article after all.

She selected a slice of toast, forked some eggs onto her plate, then offered the tray to him.

"May I ask what changed your mind?" he asked as he took some eggs for himself. "About visiting with Paolo and Arturo, that is."

She shrugged. "I'm here to help Jennifer. I promised her before I even boarded the plane that I'd do my best to keep the press from discussing her pregnancy, at least until either Antony's work is finished or the baby arrives. If playing with Arturo and Paolo keeps the press distracted and entertains the boys at the same time, that would be wonderful."

He took a bite of eggs to hide his disappointment. She didn't mention *him*. Only his sons. Not that he expected she would, but he'd harbored a hope, deep down, that he'd been part of her decision, even if nothing could come of it.

She flashed him a low-key smile as she set the tray back in the center of the table. "Your sons really are sweet."

He had to laugh at that. "You do realize my sons are the same boys who struck you with a boomerang yesterday?"

That elicited a genuine smile. "They don't plan to throw anything else at me, do they?"

"I hope not." He took a sip of his coffee before adding, "They received it from the Australian ambassador when he was visiting my father last week. I placed it on a high shelf and warned them not to use it unless I am present and tell them it is safe to do so. Obviously, that did not stop them. So please, be careful."

"I'll know to duck next time."

He cleared his throat. "I planned to take the boys to the zoo this afternoon as a final outing before school begins tomorrow. However, I was not sure that would be wise after the media coverage at the hospital yesterday. There is little chance we could visit undisturbed. And the weather today...what is the word for the prediction?"

"The weather forecast?"

"Forecast," he relegated the word to memory. "Yes, thank you. The forecast is for rain. But if you have any ideas for activities, I should like to hear them."

Her coffee cup hit the saucer so hard he feared it would shatter. "Today? You want me to go with you?"

"Unless you have plans with Jennifer, of course."

Pia shook her head. "She's planning to sort through her photos and put them in albums today, since she can do that in bed. I got everything out for her, so I think she's set. I just didn't think you'd want me to jump right in today."

He frowned. Jump in? What made her so nervous about a simple day playing with children?

Or was it because he was going along, despite the fact she dismissed what passed between them by saying it wouldn't happen again?

Finally, he said, "It is up to you, Pia. But I would enjoy it if you could join me and the children."

"You have no official engagements today?"

"After I dismissed Mona yesterday, I rearranged my schedule so I could care for the boys for the next week or two. That should give me sufficient time to find a new nanny."

She sat straighter in her chair and lifted her chin a notch, as if

resolving to tackle a difficult task. "All right. Let's plan something to
do today."

"If you are certain." He hoped she didn't view spending time with
him as an obligation. Why else did it seem she had to draw on
willpower before accepting his invitation?

"Of course I'm certain. What did you have in mind?"

He thought for a moment. "Outdoor activities will not be feasible,
unfortunately. Perhaps they would enjoy the museum?"

"Kind of public, don't you think?"

"Perhaps, though not as likely to attract reporters as the zoo."

"True. But Jennifer mentioned that she was teaching Arturo how
to play checkers. Maybe we could find a new game to teach them.
Something fun for a rainy day. My guess is the thing they want most
is to spend time with you. Nothing formal, just a free day where they
can talk and horse around, instead of going on an organized outing
like visiting the zoo or a museum."

With a mischievous gleam in her eye, she added, "Speaking of
formal, I'm going to teach you about using English contractions."

He stared at her for a moment, struck by a moment of clarity.
She'd hit on exactly the problem he'd had with his sons. While
Lucrezia ensured the boys had music lessons and participated in other
enriching activities, she'd always given Arturo and Paolo plenty of
free time. They'd stay in the playroom for hours doing nothing in
particular, or take long walks through the palace gardens. Yet ever
since Lucrezia died, in his attempts to show the boys he cared for
them more than his royal duties, he'd scheduled activities for every
moment of their time together. And worse, those activities were
almost always in public.

The time he had with them was limited, and he'd felt required to
make the most of each moment. But perhaps quiet time—private,
unplanned time—was what they craved.

Pia's soft voice interrupted his thoughts. "I'm sorry. Your English is
great, especially considering you didn't attend college in the States
like Prince Marco and Princess Isabella did. I shouldn't tease you

about it. And I really shouldn't assume anything about your children, much less open my mouth about them. I'm always putting my foot—"

"No, I appreciate your" —he searched his mind, trying to find the right word before finishing— "candor. In fact, I believe you are right. A day with nothing specific on the agenda might be fun."

They were interrupted by a staff member who cleared their dishes and replaced the empty coffee pot with a new one after refilling their cups. They each sat back from the table, allowing the man to do his job. Once he carried the last of the dishes into the kitchen and Federico and Pia were alone again, the prince leaned forward. "So, what type of activities *shouldn't* we plan?"

At an amused chuckle from Pia, he added, "English I can learn, though I often second-guess myself before speaking. But I do not believe I know how to *not* plan. I fear it is an ingrained habit."

"Well, I'm the expert of not planning. When we worked at the Haffali camp, Jennifer was the one who drew up each day's schedule and kept the whole place pulled together. All I had to do was follow a checklist and make sure the important items were completed."

He leaned back in his chair. He wouldn't have guessed that, despite her usually scruffy appearance. "Knowing your mother's superior planning skills, I thought you would be the regimented one."

Pia flinched, and he realized he'd said something hurtful. Perhaps Sabrina Renati had criticized her daughter's managerial abilities?

Pia's voice was bubbly, however, when she responded. "You know my mother?"

"I do," he replied, deciding to ignore the discomfort he'd sensed in her. "Our fathers were classmates. When your father passed away and your mother opened her business, my father was one of the first to hire her to plan a party."

"I didn't know that." She fiddled with her napkin, then apparently realized what she was doing and stilled her hands. "I'm sure it helped her establish a good reputation. That was kind of him."

"She earned it," Federico replied, and he meant it. "Sabrina is one of the most respected and in-demand event planners in southern Europe. My father and Antony continue to use her. In fact, the king hoped to book her for this weekend, when we host our annual ball to support juvenile diabetes research."

A vertical crease formed between her brows. "My mother is coming here?"

"Unfortunately, no. When my father spoke with her a few months ago, she had already accepted an assignment in Berlin, arranging a three-day arts festival for the German chancellor." A light laugh escaped him. "It is not often that my father is turned down. He was quite disappointed."

Pia nodded, but her gaze remained lowered. "She hasn't been home the past few weeks, but I wasn't sure where she'd gone."

Her tone made Federico wonder if Sabrina's presence—or lack thereof—in San Rimini influenced her decision to stay with Jennifer.

Pia glanced back up at him, though the movement seemed to take mental effort. "I imagine the king found someone else?"

"He did." Realizing that she wasn't fond of the subject, he gestured toward the door. "The boys had an early music lesson. Shall we see if they are finished?"

"Sure."

Pia pushed away from the table as he said, "So, what *do* we do with them?"

"Have you asked them?"

He raised an eyebrow. "It did not occur to me. My parents certainly never asked me."

"Well, you might discover you like their ideas."

"I AM NOT sure I like this idea." Federico rifled through Arturo's closet, shaking his head at the jumble of clothing as he searched for the boy's yellow raincoat. Even the housekeeping staff seemed unable to keep up with the boys and their messes lately.

Beside him, Pia checked the size tag in a blue raincoat that Teodora had offered to lend her and made a small sound of approval before pulling it on.

Federico finally glimpsed of a splash of yellow wedged toward the rear of Arturo's sizable closet. After fishing out the raincoat, he turned to Pia. "It is not considered proper for royal children to run about in the rain. They might catch cold."

"That's a myth," Pia knelt to help Paolo thread one of his arms through the sleeve of his sunshine yellow one before raising a brow in surprise at the first part of Federico's statement. "Wait. You never played in the rain as a child? Or splashed in puddles? Ever?"

"You have met my father, King Eduardo? No, it was not something he would permit, particularly in those days." A lighthearted laugh escaped him. "Even so, it is not something I believed I would permit, either."

"But Papa, you said we could do anything we wanted!" Paolo stared at his father in alarm.

"We're going, Paolo. Right, Papa?" Arturo shot his father a questioning look even as he stuffed his stockinged feet into a pair of black galoshes, intent on getting as far along in the process as possible before Federico changed his mind about their outdoor excursion.

Federico ruffled Arturo's hair. "Nonno has relaxed somewhat over the years. Perhaps, if I were a child now, he would allow it. And I gave you my word, yes?"

"Yes!" both boys yelled, giving each other an awkward fist bump and nearly bowling Pia over in their scramble to get outdoors.

Less than five minutes later, however, Pia found herself starting to see things from Federico's perspective. The boys' idea of playing in the rain might not be such a good idea, though she disagreed with Federico about the boys' catching cold. Rather, she suspected they'd ruin their outfits despite their raincoats. Or worse, get hurt, given the slippery, rain-soaked grass.

The moment they'd exited the rear palace doors and taken the steps leading to the garden, Arturo and Paolo tore ahead of the adults. Pia feared one—or both—of the boys might tumble the whole way down, judging from the combination of their speed, the rain-slicked steps, and their tendency to turn their heads as they ran to see if their father was watching.

Paolo let out a whoop as he reached the bottom, then jumped off the final step, landing squarely in a puddle. Water and gobs of mud splashed onto his galoshes and khaki cargo pants. Pia glanced at Federico, expecting to see disapproval on his face. Her heart lifted, however, when he patted the pockets of his trench coat and cursed himself for not having his phone or a camera on hand to capture the event.

Arturo screamed with delight, also having gauged his father's reaction to Paolo's playful jump, then took the same leap off the bottom step, soaking Paolo with muddy rainwater. The boys kicked water at each other and held their hands out, trying to deflect each other's splashes, until Federico reached the bottom of the stairs and urged them out of the puddle, onto a drier section of the gravel drive separating the palace from the garden. "Boys, boys! Shall we show Ms. Renati the swings?"

"Come see!" Arturo skipped ahead, eyeing his father before skirting another puddle, which had formed in a tire rut. He yelled over his shoulder for Paolo to catch him, then made his way onto a smaller gravel path, this one clearly intended for walking, that led through the palace's formal rose garden.

"Are you prepared to run?" Federico asked Pia as he quickened his pace.

"Do I have a choice?" Pia took a stutter step to catch Federico, thinking that while she was dressed for chasing children, in relaxed clothes and a raincoat, Federico was not. He hadn't changed out of the black slacks, gunmetal tie, and light gray shirt he'd worn to breakfast. Instead of wearing a raincoat, he'd donned a double-breasted black trench coat, far more appropriate for his usual government duties than for an afternoon playing with children in a rainy garden. She glanced down at his pristine black wing tips as he stepped over a puddle to scoop up Paolo with one arm.

Good thing the prince was filthy rich, because his polished shoes probably wouldn't survive the day.

Pia jogged alongside Federico, who balanced a giggling Paolo on his hip. They allowed Arturo to lead the way along the twisting gravel path through the rose garden. Despite their pace, Pia savored the refreshing sensation of the soft, warm rain against her face and the peppery scent of the perfectly manicured boxwood. Even the perfume of the roses in early autumn bloom seemed enhanced by the falling rain.

At last they rounded a corner at the far end of the garden, where the boxwood-bordered gravel path emptied onto the palace's long, grassy lawn. As Arturo raced ahead, she realized a swingset had been tucked under the protective covering of two large trees. Evergreens dotted the surrounding area, creating a natural shield so neither those in the public areas of the palace nor those walking along San Rimini's cobblestoned streets, which bordered the property's wrought iron fence, could see the play area.

"You have so much privacy here," she marveled. "I didn't believe that was possible on the palace grounds."

"You'd be surprised," he replied as he set down Paolo, then watched the boy follow his older brother to the swingset and hoist himself into a swing. "My mother made a real effort to provide us with time away from the cameras. She selected this site and designed the plantings for seclusion. Antony and I practically lived in these swings as children. Later, Marco came here, when he wasn't off hiding somewhere in the rose garden."

"What about your sister?"

He shrugged as he gave Paolo a push. "Isabella liked to read, even as a very young child. She always had a book with her when we came here and usually sat on the grass instead of playing. Later, my mother encouraged Isabella to explore the medieval section of the palace. I think, since Isabella was the only girl and quieter than the rest of us, my mother wanted her to have a place of her own. She allowed her to use one of the rooms in the old keep as a reading spot."

Pia leaned forward to help Arturo twist the ropes of his swing. When she let go of the ropes, allowing them to untwist, he shrieked with joy, leaning back and staring at the overcast sky as it spun above him.

Pia returned Arturo's exuberant grin, but inside, she felt a stab of envy for Federico's upbringing. What she would have given for a hideaway of her own, as Isabella had. Or a parent who'd come outside with her, push her in a swing, or race with her along garden pathways.

She took a step back from where she'd been twisting Arturo and watched as the boy pumped his legs, driving the swing higher and higher. She looked sideways at Federico. He'd moved away from Paolo, who screamed that he'd swing as high as his older brother. She wondered if he was going too high, but Federico didn't seem bothered.

"The queen must have been a wonderful mother to you," she commented. Despite her own wistfulness, Pia realized that Federico's loving upbringing probably helped make him a better father.

"She was. It's been nearly eight years now, and I still miss her. She died much too early. She knew we had Arturo on the way, but didn't live long enough to meet him." He lowered his voice, so Arturo and Paolo wouldn't hear. "I cannot imagine if I had lost her at the age my sons are now. My life would have been quite different."

"Your father would have worked extra hard to ensure you enjoyed your childhood," Pia assured him. "There's no substitute for having two loving parents, but I think, had your father been in your situation, he would have made the same effort you've made since Lucrezia passed away. And you would have appreciated it, just as your sons will."

Federico nodded, but the lines at the edges of his eyes seemed a notch deeper, and she suspected the knowledge that his children had been deprived of their mother would always cause him pain. A yell from Arturo distracted him from their conversation. Before Pia determined the cause, Federico leaped away from her, lunging past Paolo toward Arturo.

To her horror, Pia realized that Arturo had decided to leap from the swing and that he was far too high in the air to do so safely. Pia stood rooted to the spot, her stomach clenched in fear as Federico reached out for his son, grabbing him and rolling backward to break Arturo's fall just before the boy hit the ground.

"Arturo!" Federico scolded once he'd caught his breath. "How many times have I asked you not to jump if the swing is so high?"

Arturo pulled a face. "I was six when you said that. Now I'm seven and a half!"

"It does not matter. You must never jump if your feet are higher than my head. You can get hurt. Especially on wet grass."

"I didn't jump, Papa! Look at me!" Paolo giggled and continued to pump his swing higher, oblivious to the risk Arturo had taken.

"That's good, Paolo," Pia finally managed to open her mouth and speak while Federico frowned at Arturo. "It's fun, isn't it?"

The little boy gave a one-sided shrug and grinned, happy he wasn't the one in trouble. Pia didn't share Paolo's glee, however. The sight of Arturo launching himself from the swing, his legs kicking through the air and his arms splayed to stop himself from the inevitable fall forward, took her right back to the afternoon of her babysitting accident.

A hard knot lodged in her throat. Federico had moved with a parent's innate sense of protection, managing to keep his son from a bad fall. Yet she'd stood there, unmoving, her heart beating so fast she thought it would burst through her chest. All these years and scads of emergency training later, and she still hadn't overcome her inability to prevent a child's accident.

Arturo gave his father a sheepish look that Pia suspected wasn't entirely heartfelt, apologized, then climbed back on his swing.

"If you do that again, no swings for a month, Arturo. Do you understand?"

"Yes, Papa," he said as he began to pump his legs again. "I won't jump."

"Are you all right?" Pia asked Federico when she noticed he wasn't getting up.

He planted both hands on the grass and levered himself to stand. "Oh, I am quite all right. Merely annoyed. They like to skirt the rules." He shook his head, but a smile played at his lips as he dropped his voice to a confidential level and added, "At least Arturo does. I must keep an eye on him at all times. He is too much like my brother

Marco, I fear. Always testing, trying to determine how far he can push before he is disciplined."

"He'd give me a heart attack if he were my son. You handled that quite calmly."

"Only because I am used to it." Federico took a step forward to help Paolo out of his swing, then boosted him onto the ladder leading to the short slide attached to the end of the swingset.

When the prince returned to Pia's side, he added, "Their willingness to test boundaries can be stressful, but it is also their appeal. Everything is predictable in my life except the boys, and there are days I take pleasure in that."

Pia murmured her agreement, but privately, she wasn't sure she'd feel the same way, were she in Federico's place. Kids provided plenty of excitement without their tendency toward recklessness.

Still, her admiration for Federico rose a notch for his ability to appreciate his children's natural playfulness. How little credit she'd given him the day she arrived in San Rimini, daring to call his affection for his children into question as they'd entered the palace grounds in the back of the Mercedes and heard his sons' laughter. She couldn't have been more off the mark, and she'd been wrong to judge him by her own insecurities.

Arturo took a headfirst slide behind Paolo, then ran forward and grabbed his father's arm. "Papa, can we play hide and seek in the garden?"

"Only if you promise to stay within this area," Federico warned. "Do not go past the fountain. I must know where you are at all times."

Paolo's brow wrinkled. "We can't play hide and seek if you know where we are. That's not fair."

"You know what he means," Arturo rolled his eyes heavenward. "We can only hide in this section, and we can't leave it. It wouldn't be safe."

Paolo brightened. "Okay! Find me, Papa! You're it!"

With that, he took off, his steps awkward as he crossed the wet grass in his galoshes, with his raincoat ending below his knees and cutting his steps short. When he reached the edge of the lawn, he spun to face the adults. "Ms. Renati can hide too, *si?*"

"*Si,*" Federico agreed, then waved Pia ahead. "Go hide."

Whether the smile pulling at her lips was from relief at leaving the swings—and the memories they stirred in her—or at her amusement over being asked to hide by Paolo, who'd been so shy with her after the boomerang incident, she wasn't certain. But without a word to Federico, she scampered after the boys.

Once they'd left Federico's line of sight, Paolo stopped running and twisted his head to look up at Pia. "I know a really good hiding place. Would you like to hide with me?"

How could she resist? "Show me."

His brown eyes twinkled with excitement as he grabbed her hand. "Through here."

He led her down a side path, under a rose-covered arbor, then surprised her by pulling her to the outside of the arch and onto a small patch of grass growing between the arbor and a row of boxwood hedges. "Papa will never look here," he promised.

"It's a very good spot," she whispered, wiping a drop of rain off Paolo's pink nose as they crouched low. "As long as you don't get poked by the thorns."

"I know! The roses are sharp." He thrust out one of his tiny hands, showing her a long red mark. "I got stuck last week. Didn't hurt, though."

"That looks bad, Paolo."

"The nanny cleaned it and put a bandage on it. Papa checked it and he said it was all right."

Paolo leaned forward and poked his fingers through the crossbars of the trellis, careful to avoid the thorny canes, and created a hole so he could see the path where it passed under the arbor. Arturo skidded by and made a face in Paolo's direction, clearly having had the same idea as his younger brother. Paolo giggled while Arturo looked back, listening for his father, then hid on the opposite side of the arbor.

"Mamma found this hiding place for me when I was little," he whispered. "Signorina Fennini didn't ever find me when I hid here!"

Pia smiled at the pink-faced boy beside her, who obviously thought he'd grown from a little boy into a big one, but felt another pang of guilt over the nanny's dismissal. She wondered how much the boys had liked Mona. Clearly not as much as they adored their mother, though Pia found it difficult to imagine fashion-forward Lucrezia running through the arbor playing hide and seek, let alone crouching in the tiny space she and Paolo now occupied on the side of the arbor.

Still, she was glad the boys remembered their mother fondly. Even though only two years had passed since Lucrezia's death—not long in an adult's memory—two years constituted eons in little kid time.

As footsteps approached on the path they'd just left, however, Pia's thoughts turned to Federico. From her position, she could see past the thick rose canes through a gap in the trellis. Mud spatters covered Federico's shoes and the cuffs of his slacks, and she smiled to herself as he swiped a hand over his dark, wet hair. Federico needed to get messy, to cut loose and do something unscheduled, perhaps even more than his sons needed it.

And did the prince's blue eyes shine brighter in the rain, or what?

"Arturo, Paolo," the prince called out in a sing-songy tone she thought him incapable of, given his rich masculine voice and regal bearing. "Ready or not, here I come!"

Paolo moved closer to Pia, huddling against her body and giggling. A tiny smile tugged at the corners of Federico's mouth, but he continued along the path, calling for the boys and pretending not to have heard.

He moved far enough past the arbor and out of sight, though not out of earshot. He continued to call for the boys as he followed the circular path through the rose garden, mock panic filling his voice at his inability to find anyone.

She glanced down at Paolo's excited face, flashing him a grin. "This is fun, isn't it?"

He nodded. "Are you going to play with us again tomorrow? We only have a half day of school because it's the first day."

"We'll have to see. I hope so." Aside from Arturo trying to give her heart failure when he'd leaped from the swing, she was having a good time, exactly as Jennifer had predicted. And Arturo's jump hadn't been so bad, really. If anything, witnessing a few of the boys' mishaps might convince her that kids were more resilient than she'd allowed herself to believe.

"I wish you would." Paolo's face filled with a child's sincerity. "My mamma died, and I really want one I can play with. It would make Papa happy."

Pia started to answer, but clamped her mouth shut. How could she respond to such a heartbreaking, yet innocent, request?

"Come on," Paolo grabbed her arm and urged her to stand, his thoughts obviously skittering from one idea to the next faster than hers. "Papa will return soon. We have to hide somewhere he has already looked."

"Is that fair?"

He shrugged, his eyes sparkling with mischief. "Arturo does it all the time."

She shook her head in amusement, but followed him down the path. Paolo's footsteps were loud enough as he crunched through the gravel in his galoshes that Federico had to hear him running. She wondered how long it would be before he found them.

The idea of being found by Federico while she hid between rows of fragrant roses and boxwood, even though a child stood at her hip, sent her pulse racing.

She sucked in a deep lungful of the moist garden air, then exhaled. What was wrong with her? She had no right imagining any type of adventures with Federico. She had to view him as Paolo and Arturo's father. A man whose children needed stability, not an interloper coming in and getting hot and heavy with their dad then taking off for Africa, to an area where she'd be lucky to have consistent phone service, much less personal contact with him. Part of her rationale for joining them this afternoon was to see Federico from a different perspective—a practical one—not to develop an even deeper crush.

Thoughts of Federico faded when Paolo took a sharp corner, bringing them face-to-face with a large fountain. Pia stopped short, her mouth opening in a quiet O. Never in her life had she seen anything so breathtaking.

A low stone lip separated the water of the pool from the path. In the center stood a large sculpture of an opening flower, with water shooting from the top in a dozen different directions. Statues of sprightly woodland nymphs graced each of the flower's leaf sets, spraying water down into the pool from carved vases, as if the women had been commanded to do so by the gods. The water rippled with life, and she noticed several Euros scattered along the bottom—wishes made by the royal family, their aristocratic guests, or their staff, who were the only people permitted in this area of the garden. She'd had access to this area during Jennifer's wedding reception, but hadn't made it here.

"Do you like it?" Paolo asked.

"It's beautiful." Even in the rain, the sound of the cascading water brought a serenity to the garden that she wouldn't have thought one could find in the center of a busy European city. She studied the graceful arcs of water tumbling into the pool for a moment before adding, "But didn't your father say that we shouldn't go past the fountain? Why don't we turn around and—"

Where had Paolo gone?

She glanced toward the path behind her, wondering how he'd walked away without her hearing his steps in the gravel.

Then she heard a splash. When she turned and saw Paolo, her body chilled. "Paolo! *Paolo!*"

The little boy lay facedown in the water, his bright raincoat floating around him. Neither his arms nor his legs moved.

CHAPTER 6

PIA LEAPED over the low edge of the pool and jogged through the water toward Paolo's inert form, her heart thudding so hard she felt it in her ears.

Please, please, please, don't let him be dead!

She lunged forward, frantic with worry, though at the same time she knew he couldn't have drowned so quickly. Just as she grabbed the back of Paolo's coat, he popped up, laughing and spitting water at her even as she screamed.

"Fooled you!" His face split into a huge smile and his eyes sparkled with childlike delight.

Pia sat back in the water, soaking herself to the bone, and closed her eyes in relief. "Paolo, you scared me to death. Please don't do that again."

"Wasn't it funny? You thought I fell in!"

"Paolo!" Federico's voice boomed behind them, his commanding tone that of a man who expected to be obeyed. "Get out of the water! *Adesso!*"

Paolo stiffened in surprise, unhappy his father witnessed his impromptu swim. He glanced at Pia before wading to the edge, his face flaming as he approached Federico.

The prince's hardened expression left no doubt as to the seriousness of Paolo's transgression. "You must never, ever go in the fountain, Paolo."

"I just wanted to trick Ms. Renati." His voice hitched, though he managed to hold back his tears. "I was being funny."

"Playing in the fountain is dangerous, not funny." He slid a pointed look at Pia, which Paolo followed. "Ms. Renati thinks you're funny just the way you are, so no more tricks. *Capisce?*"

He sniffed as he shoved his wet locks back from his face. "I'm sorry, Papa. I won't do it again."

"Good. I trust you to keep your word. Now, you must apologize to Ms. Renati."

Paolo did so, and it was heartfelt. Federico nodded his approval, then placed his palm on top of Paolo's dripping head. "Playtime outside is over for today. We must get you some dry clothes."

"Do we have to?"

Federico needed only to raise his eyebrows to quiet further protest. Paolo ducked from under his father's hand and clambered out of the fountain.

"Papa! You didn't find me!"

Pia stood and looked down the path toward the sound of Arturo's aggravated voice as she moved away from the center of the fountain and tried to settle her nerves.

"You must have found a very good hiding place," Federico said once Arturo was closer. "Next time, make it easier. I am not as good at this game as you."

Arturo's irritation turned to a smile, but Federico spun both boys toward the rear doors of the palace. "Time to change out of these wet clothes. We have enjoyed enough adventures outdoors for today."

"Can we watch my airplane show?" Paolo asked. "*Per favore?*"

"No, Papa, I want Spongebob," Arturo pleaded, grabbing Federico's arm. "You promised me this morning."

"Since both of you disobeyed me today, we shall skip the television. Perhaps tomorrow."

The boys grumbled, but kept it under their breath. Federico turned to Pia, his gaze softening as he offered her a hand. She took it, appreciating his firm hold as she stepped over the fountain's slippery edge and onto the gravel path.

"I am truly sorry, Pia. Paolo knows better. I do not know what possessed him."

A need for attention, if she had to guess. But she said, "It's all right. I haven't had a good dunking in a while. Deep down, I knew he was safe. He was only in the fountain a few seconds when I went in after him."

"You should not have had a dunking today," he said, then let go of her hand and brushed a few soggy curls away from her bandage. He frowned, then apparently deemed the bandage fine because he raised his face to the sky for a moment. "The damp of the rain is bad enough."

"The rain's not so bad. It makes the whole garden smell fresh. Besides, it's nice to have the whole place to ourselves."

"That is true. I rarely have time alone. Well, you understand what I mean. Time away from where I am judged." He touched her shoulder briefly, then his blue eyes met hers, and they held the same depth of emotion she'd seen in the instant before he'd kissed her in the hospital hallway. Not the first, gentle kiss, but the second. The heated one.

His thoughts must have traveled the same route as hers, because he took a step back, as if deciding their closeness walked a perilous line. He gestured toward his sons, indicating that perhaps he and Pia should catch up.

They walked side by side along the path, following the drenched boys, who seemed to find every puddle on their way to the stairs. It was all too easy to imagine her cold hand enveloped in his larger one, or the thrill of having him pull her under the arbor for a clandestine kiss.

She tried to focus on the path, the roses. Anything but Federico.

"Today was good for me, despite the boys' behavior." Federico said, glancing sideways at her as the rear doors of the palace came into view at the end of the garden path. "Lucrezia and I were often away during the daylight hours, so we rarely had time with them in the garden. It has usually been their nannies. Now I realize that was a mistake."

His observation surprised her. "Paolo gave me the impression Lucrezia played hide and seek with him. That she showed him the hiding spot in the arbor." She found herself grinning as she added, "which was wonderful of you to overlook, by the way."

He returned the smile. "Pretending I cannot find them is part of the game. But no, I do not believe Lucrezia played hide and seek with them. It was not her way. She preferred to read to the boys or play board games indoors when she wasn't at an engagement."

"This was probably a nice change for them." She hoped she sounded diplomatic. If Paolo felt compelled to lie, or at least to imagine he'd played outdoors with his mother, then Lucrezia's death probably still affected the little boy more than Federico realized. Enough that Paolo had asked her if she'd be his new mother.

The prince cleared his throat. "I assume that you have read some of San Rimini's tabloids over the years?"

What sparked that question? "From time to time when I'm in San Rimini. At the hairdresser, places like that. Not as a habit, though." She slid him a sideways glance. "Why?"

"Then you may know that I am often called 'Prince Perfect.'"

She barely managed to suppress her grin. His expression showed his disdain for the nickname. To put him at ease, she teased, "Oh, I may have seen that nickname attached to you once or twice. Or wait…was that about Marco? With a name like Prince Perfect, it could be Marco." She pretended to consider it for a moment before shaking her head and asking, "Are you sure they meant you?"

She stared pointedly at the caked mud on his shoes and slacks, then tried not to laugh at the pretended pain on his face.

Unable to maintain his composure, Federico released a roar of laughter, one that carried far enough for Arturo and Paolo to glance back to see what caused it. Pia loved seeing the prince relaxed at long last. He put on such a stiff, formal front to the world, but underneath, he possessed both humor and heart.

"It most assuredly was not about Marco," he said between laughs. "Only Marco is convinced of his own perfection."

"Perhaps Amanda as well."

"Oh, she's well aware of his imperfections. Fortunately for Marco, she loves him in spite of them."

He swiped absently at a wet leaf that clung to the side of his pants and angled his head to look at her, his features turning serious. "I despise that they call me Prince Perfect."

"Why?" She wanted to argue that he really was the perfect prince. Caring, honorable, always putting others before himself—a whole country before himself—but if she uttered that opinion, it also meant admitting the strength of her attraction.

Careful to choose the right words, she added, "I thought they called you Prince Perfect because you're the model of all a San Riminian prince should be. You know what to say and when, your actions reflect your words, and you've never given the media the slightest scandal to hang a story on. You're a perfect representative of our country, and I'm sure you've worked hard to maintain that reputation." She shot him an evil grin. "I bet it drives those muckrakers nuts."

"Muck—? Ah, yes. The scandal reporters. I am certain it does. But I am not perfect. Far from it. I used to believe I was a good role model. I prided myself on my behavior. But now, well, now I know better." His gaze slipped to the boys, who stood at the bottom of the palace steps, comparing the amount of mud coating their once-clean galoshes. "For instance, I have not been a perfect father since Lucrezia died, and that is the most important role in the world. I thought I was doing the right thing, taking them on outings. Formal outings. But I felt off" — he tapped his chest— "in here. Now I understand why."

He stopped walking, and Pia stopped, too, aware that he wanted her undivided attention. "I never realized how much Arturo and Paolo needed time just to be boys, with nothing to do but play, and to do that with their own father, instead of a nanny."

"First, no one is a perfect parent, even the people who write parenting books. And second, you have more obligations than the typical parent. Cut yourself some slack." She kept her tone breezy, hoping Federico wouldn't take himself quite so seriously. "But given that you've felt off, make the changes that resonate with you. Perhaps adjust your schedule so you can spend time with them each afternoon, and let them know you'll continue to make time for them, even after you find a nanny." A nanny who'd do any number of fun things with the boys, like play tag, teach them magic tricks, or build tents out of blankets.

The mental image of another woman laughing with the boys gave her a quick flare of jealousy.

"I'm beginning to understand." To Pia's surprise, Federico reached out and grabbed her hand. Despite the dampness of the palace gardens, his fingers radiated warmth and strength. "But I would not have understood it without you. Thank you."

"It was nothing," she replied, her voice huskier than she'd intended. Nothing that a lifetime of being ignored by her own mother hadn't taught her. Kids needed love. And time.

For a brief moment, as Federico's fingers interlaced with hers, she wished she could do something special for the boys. Wished she could hug away all Paolo's hurts, make him realize he didn't have to fake drowning or concoct stories about his late mother to get attention. Take Arturo someplace he could throw his boomerang with no restraints.

"It was something." Federico gave her hand a squeeze, then let go and began to walk again, unwilling to let the boys stand in the rain much longer. "You know, Pia, you will make a wonderful wife and mother someday. I hope your future husband and children realize their good fortune."

She forced herself to smile her thanks, but before she could think of what to say, Federico jogged ahead of her to ensnare his giggling boys, one in each arm. Her insides went hollow as she watched them. To daydream of Federico and his boys was more dangerous than taking a boomerang to the skull.

His words—though meant as a compliment—also served as a dismissal of any potential for a relationship.

She mentally castigated herself for wanting him, then concentrated on her foot placement as she ascended the wet stairs. Despite what had happened in the hospital, he'd made it clear he wasn't ready for a relationship. As much as her heart screamed for that not to be true, he'd apparently meant it. Couple that with her inner panic when Arturo flew from the swing, or when Paolo played a simple joke...she bit down on the inside of her lip to stifle a sigh. As much as part of her wanted to be a mother, to know the joy Federico experienced every time he held his sons, it wasn't in her stars.

It was a chance none of them, least of all the children, could afford to take. She couldn't go through that hurt again.

———

WHY COULD he not keep his thoughts to himself?

Federico jammed Arturo's wet coat onto a hook with more force than necessary, then strode into the boys' small bathroom for a towel to dry their hair. He spent his whole life learning to speak when appropriate, and to hold his tongue when it would better serve him, his family, or his country.

What had possessed him to blurt out to Pia that she would make some lucky man a good wife? It was true, of course—Pia exuded a blend of practicality and charm anyone would love—but she'd likely taken the statement as a rejection, given the attraction between them and the mind-blowing kiss they'd shared less than twenty-four hours ago.

He gritted his teeth. He'd said it out of a primal instinct to protect himself. He'd confused the appreciation of a woman with love before and did not care to do it again. Maybe he'd thought that saying the words aloud would prove nothing existed between them.

But it did exist. The connection was strong enough to feel tangible.

Then there was his comment about Pia being a mother, and the hurt that he'd glimpsed on her face before he turned away to scoop up the boys. She'd been careful to hide it, but that look shot straight to his gut.

Now he wondered if her odd behavior at breakfast and her look of dread when Arturo leaped from the swing or when Paolo climbed in the fountain resulted from an inability to bear children. He'd witnessed a similar pained expression on the faces of friends who'd had difficulty conceiving. Invariably, they worried more about children's bumps and bruises than other parents, to whom children seemed more resilient. If not infertility, then something else had set Pia's emotions on edge when it came to children. He hadn't imagined that flash of torment.

He truly was no Prince Perfect. It shouldn't have surprised him when Pia excused herself to return to Jennifer's apartment the moment they made it indoors, despite the fact he had offered her dry clothes and dinner. It wasn't a need to check on Jennifer, as she had claimed. He could see that much in the way she averted her eyes, in the subtle drop of her shoulders.

And he'd heard it in her final words, when she'd wished him good luck with his effort to find a nanny.

He should take the hint. Instead, he wanted to know what was behind that torment.

"Papa?" Paolo poked his head around the bathroom door. "Did you find my towel?"

"I have it here." He tried not to think about Pia as he fluffed Paolo's short, dark hair, which was much like his own, yet with Lucrezia's eyes peeping out underneath. "Find your pajamas, Paolo, and bring them to the bathroom. You smell like mud and rain. Tonight you shall have your bath before dinner."

"With bubbles?"

Federico pretended to have a hard time deciding, but a pleading look from Paolo made him smile. "All right."

"Papa, today was fun."

"I am glad you thought so."

"We can do it again sometime?"

"I would like that."

"And will Ms. Renati be my new mamma?"

Federico's spine stiffened. "Why do you ask that?"

Paolo shrugged. "I like her. She's nice. I told her it would be good if she could be my mamma."

An expletive roared through Federico's brain, but he managed to sound nonchalant as he asked, "You did?"

When Paolo nodded, Federico asked, "What did she say?"

The little boy's mouth screwed up. "I don't remember. I wanted to show her the fountain. There were coins in it, but I didn't take any. Can I wear my frog pajamas?"

"Of course."

Paolo bolted from the bathroom to find them.

He swiped Paolo's towel off the floor. He must have dropped it when Paolo asked his impossible question.

Good thing Paolo was easily distracted. Pia would have a longer memory.

As soon as he finished bathing the boys, he'd send a note to his assistant about contacting the nanny service, as Pia suggested. Then, the next time he saw Pia, he'd discover her secrets and apologize for his heartless comments.

As he'd told Paolo, the day had been too much fun not to repeat. He needed to make certain that happened.

"You're soaked!" Jennifer's eyes were nearly as wide as her ever-spreading midsection when Pia entered the apartment. Pia took off her borrowed coat and hung it in the adjoining bathroom, hoping she hadn't dripped on any of the expensive rugs. She'd brushed off as much water as possible when she'd entered the palace, and had left her sodden footwear outside Jennifer's door, but now she wondered if she should have gone to her guest room before checking on her friend.

Jennifer's gaze lit on Pia's wet hair and clothes as she emerged from the bathroom. "I didn't mean that you should go to the beach today."

"We didn't. The boys wanted to play in the garden, splash around in puddles, that sort of thing."

Jennifer replaced the lid on a box of photographs, then swooped aside a pile of photo adhesive, scrapbook pages, and specialty markers to make room for Pia to sit on the bed beside her. Pia begged off, gesturing at her wet clothes. "I should change first. Thanks to Paolo, I got wetter than I intended."

"Was it fun?"

"It was."

Jennifer beamed. "I love it when I get to say, 'I told you so.' I bet the boys loved it. Federico would never go puddle jumping."

When Pia couldn't hide her smile, Jennifer's jaw dropped. "Wait. *Federico* went outside with you? In the rain? You have got to be kidding! How did you convince him? Did he declare an emergency when he realized his designer suit would get wet? Or did he hold an umbrella over himself the whole time?"

"He didn't carry an umbrella, he didn't declare an emergency, and he didn't need convincing. Not by me, at least. The boys said that's what they wanted to do today, so he went."

"Unbelievable." Jennifer dropped the photo paraphernalia into a storage box, then put her hands to the small of her back, massaging her muscles while she studied Pia. "It's about time. He needed to do something entertaining. I swear, I've hardly seen him crack a smile since Lucrezia passed away. He's changed so much, it's hard to believe he's the same man I met when I first visited the palace. He's always been the epitome of class and style in public, but in private, he's witty, and he's so kind. He even told a joke the first night I met him, at the fundraiser I attended for the scholarship fund."

Jennifer shot an inquisitive look at Pia to see if she remembered her trip to San Rimini for the event, then continued at Pia's nod. "He made a crack about one of the society women in attendance—a woman who, shall we say, was less than polite to me—because he wanted to put me at ease after he witnessed her behavior. Given his public image, I never would have imagined it." She gave a one-shouldered shrug. "Anyway, I haven't seen that side of him lately. Maybe the fact that he went out in the rain with you and the kids means he's getting back to his old self."

Pia tried to contain her surprise. While she'd seen glimpses of humor, she would never peg Federico as the type to poke fun at others in his social circle, especially those important to his family's social status. She wanted to ask Jennifer more about Federico's 'old self,' but a knock at the door interrupted them. Pia moved Jennifer's storage boxes off the bed for her, then strode to the door, opening it wide to admit Antony's assistant, Harriet Hunt.

Harriet nodded in deference to Jennifer as she entered the bedroom, then handed over a stack of correspondence before turning to Pia. "Your mother just phoned. I have her holding on line three." She tilted her head toward the hallway. "I transferred the call to your room so you'd have privacy, but I can redirect the call here, if you prefer."

Pia bit back her automatic urge to decline the phone call. Jennifer didn't know how deep Pia's frustration with her own mother ran, but now wasn't the time or place to discuss it.

"No, that's not necessary, Harriet. I was about to go to my room to change into dry clothes." Pia thanked Harriet, told Jennifer she'd return shortly, then strode into the hallway and crossed to her guest room, which was located a few doors away from Antony and Jennifer's apartment.

She hesitated before answering the phone, staring at the red light next to line three on the palace's internal system. Had her mother seen the news report? Or had someone engaged in a little royal gossip and informed Sabrina Renati that her daughter was a guest of the diTalora family?

However her mother had heard, she'd chosen to call the palace rather than try Pia's cell phone.

Pia found a towel to protect the ivory silk-covered chair beside her bed, then took a deep breath, sat down, and picked up the receiver.

"Hi, Mom."

"Pia! I'm so glad I finally reached you. Why didn't you tell me you were in San Rimini? I'm in Berlin, finishing up a project, but I can catch an earlier flight if—"

"That's not necessary, Mom. Don't alter your schedule. Besides, I'm pretty busy here."

"Oh." A beat elapsed before she continued, "So what's going on? I saw you on television with Prince Federico. I didn't realize you were acquainted. I know you and Jennifer are close, but is what I saw true? Are you seeing Prince Federico?"

Sabrina's voice was filled with hope, and Pia's senses instantly went on alert. Trust her mother to be on top of every rumor in Europe, and to be thrilled at the idea of her daughter taking up with San Rimini's most famous single male.

"No, Mother. I came to see Jennifer before she has her baby. I have a new assignment starting soon in Africa, and the timing was good for me to visit her. I'm not sure what you saw on television, but I accidentally cut my head. Prince Federico was nearby when it happened, so he offered to take me to the hospital. That's the whole story."

"Oh. The report made it sound like something more."

"Don't sound so disappointed, Mom."

"It's not what you think, dear." Pia could easily picture her mother's exasperated expression. "I only want what's best for you. I want you to be happy."

"I am happy. I love my job."

"Trust me, a job is not enough."

Pia nearly dropped the phone. "This from the woman who loves her job more than anything? Look how much time and effort you put into it. You wouldn't do that if you didn't love what you do."

"I never said I didn't love it. But I put in the time and effort because that's what it takes to be successful in this field. That has meant a lot of sacrifices, as you well know." An audible sigh came over the line. "I wasn't exactly a model parent, but these choices in life are difficult. I had simply hoped you'd found happiness, that's all."

Pia sensed a forced cheer from her mother. "I'll be back in San Rimini day after tomorrow if you want to reach me. And I can be there before that, if you change your mind."

"I'll let you know."

"Please do." She paused a moment before asking, "Is your head all right?"

"Perfectly fine."

Another pause. "Well, you have my cell number. I love you, Pia. Enjoy your time there."

Pia hesitated before answering, "Thanks, Mom. I appreciate it. I'll talk to you soon."

After her mother said goodbye, Pia replaced the receiver and shucked off her wet clothes, dropping them into a pile on the bathroom tile, then pulled on a simple white shirt and black slacks. She intended to return to Jennifer's room, but after pulling a comb through her damp hair, she flopped on the bed and jammed her fists to her temples.

Why, why, why, did her conversation with her mother suddenly remind her of Federico and *his* situation? She shouldn't feel sympathy for her mother. Yet suddenly, guilt made her wonder if she should be more understanding of Sabrina Renati, just as she'd grown understanding, and even appreciative, of Federico's struggles as a parent.

Perhaps it was her mother's statement that she wasn't a model parent, and that she'd had to make choices.

"Would have been nice if you'd chosen a career that let you be home once in a while," Pia muttered aloud.

Of course, a world of career paths hadn't been open to her mother when she found herself widowed with a young child. Sabrina had come from a lower middle-class family, and when she'd met her husband, had opted not to complete her studies. As the wife of an aristocrat, she had only needed social and organizational skills, which she possessed in abundance.

Even Pia had to admit, the choice of a career as an event planner had been a natural one.

Just as Pia's choice, to help people in the far reaches of the globe, was a natural fit. She made life better for those who couldn't help themselves—refugees, the poor, the sick. It made her feel needed and gave her a sense of purpose she'd missed during her childhood. The more she distanced herself from her mother's high-society, busy-all-the-time lifestyle, the better. Or so she'd thought.

Pia swiped a palm over her face and pushed out of bed. As she hung her wet clothes over the shower rod to dry, she resolved to call her mother when Sabrina returned from Germany. Even though her mother couldn't change the past, maybe now that they were both adults they could become friends, or at least develop a healthier respect for each other.

Pia grabbed the notepad from her desk and jotted down a reminder to call her mother and invite her to lunch. She might not be able to work things out entirely, but at least she'd stop running from the problem.

She made sure everything in the room was straightened in case the housekeeping staff stopped by, then headed for the door. As flustered as her mother made her, it was another single parent who plagued her thoughts. Watching Federico with his children this afternoon made her more attracted to him, not less.

If she didn't back off, she'd fall hard.

"Too late," she mocked herself aloud. Good thing she'd reminded him that he still needed to find a nanny. If she spent another afternoon like this one, enjoying her time with the children—and with their too-sexy-for-words father—the next thing she knew she'd be dreaming about having children of her own with him and living happily ever after.

Like Jennifer and Antony. Jennifer really did have it all.

Now that she thought about Jen, however, Pia decided her friend had seemed more uncomfortable than usual. She'd been using her fists to grind the muscles of her lower back while they'd talked, something Pia hadn't seen her do before.

She was halfway out the door when the line rang again. She turned back inside and grabbed the receiver. Expecting her mother, she answered, "Did you forget something?"

"Pia?"

Instantly, she recognized the voice of the director of World HIV Relief. "Hi, Ellen. I'm sorry, I thought you were someone else calling me back. I don't get many calls here."

"I left a message on your cell, but thought I'd try the backup number you gave me. I hope that's all right."

"Perfectly fine. What's up?"

After a few minutes' conversation, Pia made her way back to Jennifer's room to share the news. It wasn't what she'd hoped to tell her friend. On the other hand, she reasoned, her Federico problem would be solved for her.

She couldn't exactly moon over an unattainable royal from two thousand miles away, could she?

CHAPTER 7

"Federico. Federico, wake up."

The deep voice echoed through Federico's head as if spoken through a thick fog. He shifted to his side, away from the masculine sound. On some level, he realized he was dreaming, and he didn't want a male voice there telling him what to do.

"*Mi lasci in pace,*" he mumbled. He'd been walking through the gardens with Pia, the children safely in the palace, and she'd been just about to tell him he didn't need to hire a nanny, that he should have his assistant call to cancel the interviews she'd set up in the hours after dinner that night. Her hand was on his forearm. He could feel the pressure, the urgency.

But the gravel-edged voice speaking in place of Pia's jolted his slumber.

"I will not leave you alone." This time the voice was accompanied by shaking. Federico blinked, then jerked upright, realizing he was awake, but in his private apartment rather than the garden.

"Father?" His voice emerged sounding harsh. "What is happening?"

"I apologize, but I need your help."

Federico took in the king's clothing, the same midnight navy suit he remembered his father wearing to a dinner earlier that evening, then glanced at his bedside clock, which showed a few minutes after eleven. The boys must have tired him more than he thought, because he hadn't heard his father knock, and the king never barged in on his adult children. Despite being both their parent and their monarch, he afforded them as much privacy as possible to encourage them to continue living under his roof, where high security was easier to maintain.

Whatever drove him to enter Federico's apartment rather than call had to be an emergency.

"Is it the boys?" Federico dismissed the idea before his father even answered, knowing he would have heard any disturbance with Arturo and Paolo first. "Or are you leaving the country?"

It had happened before. A few months earlier, King Eduardo boarded a last-minute flight to nearby Turkey after a devastating earthquake. He'd also done so for emergency meetings with foreign leaders during a crisis in the nearby Balkans, and again after a storm devastated parts of Cyprus, but on those occasions Antony had been present within the walls of La Rocca, and he'd been the one awakened with the news.

"The boys are fine. I need you to take Jennifer to the hospital. Pia Renati sent word to me at dinner about an hour ago. The doctor says Jennifer is in the early stages of labor, but progressing rapidly. We've decided it best not to wait until morning for her to make the trip to the hospital. There are four tour groups scheduled to go through the public areas then, and she would have little chance of leaving unnoticed. No need to make the media scrutiny concerning her pregnancy worse than it already is. I'll stay here in case Arturo and Paolo awaken before you return."

Federico frowned, but pushed aside his covers and strode to his closet to retrieve a pair of black slacks. "You do not wish Antony's driver to take her?"

"He's not on duty at the moment, and it might alert the paparazzi if I call him to the palace at this hour. It might be easier if you take your private vehicle and drive her yourself. Since my dinner guests are just departing, one more black Mercedes leaving the palace grounds won't draw attention. Pia will accompany you, and will stay at the hospital until Antony arrives."

"He is on his way?"

"I phoned him before coming to wake you. He has my plane in the Middle East, so he will wrap up what he can tonight and depart at sunrise."

Federico located a pair of socks in the same deep black as his slacks. "All right. Will you need me here, or should I stay at the hospital with Jennifer and Pia?"

"Stay if you wish, and I'll call if you're needed. I had my assistant clear my morning schedule, and Isabella and Nick arrived from New York two hours ago. The boys will be fine. I would enjoy having breakfast with them before they leave for school, and I know Isabella is eager to have them open the gifts she brought them from the States."

Opting for a casual look—for him—Federico removed a gray polo shirt from its hanger and wished he had at least a little time to shave and shower. Out of habit, he never appeared outside his room looking anything less than ready for a public appearance. And then there was Pia. As much as he shouldn't care about impressing her, particularly in the middle of the night with Jennifer's baby about to arrive, he did. The fact that he'd dreamed about her—and awakened still wanting her—proved that at least his subconscious wanted more than friendship from her. He glanced at his father. "I assume I need to leave now, or you wouldn't have come."

"Pia is helping Jennifer pack. If you'd like ten minutes for a shower, it won't be a problem." The king smiled. "I suppose I shall be a grandfather again shortly. I thought we still had a week or two to prepare for the baby's arrival."

"So did Jennifer."

A few minutes later, Federico stood in his Italian marble shower, cool sprays of water pummeling his head and forcing him back to wakefulness. As he engaged in a lightning-fast scrub, he caught himself smiling. Come tomorrow, he'd be cradling a new baby in his arms, a warm little body to remind him of the emotional births of his own children. It seemed like a lifetime ago that he and Lucrezia welcomed Arturo, and then Paolo, into the world.

He had to admit, as difficult as it was to balance his public schedule with caring for the boys, he would gladly welcome another child into his home. He envied Antony that, and the love of a wife welcoming him back to bed with open arms while the baby slept in its crib.

As he shut off the spray and toweled himself dry, another thought occurred to him, this one far more practical. Once the baby was born, it would bump him from the line of succession.

Federico looped his towel over the appropriate hook and laughed aloud, realizing that for the first time in his life, he was looking forward to a loss in prestige.

Perhaps, with an adorable child taking his place in line for the throne, and with attention focused on Jennifer and Antony as the world's most famous new parents, he could stop trying to be Prince Perfect and spend more time being a father.

Today had shown him the value of letting go, of reveling in parenthood, no matter what the media or his adherence to duty dictated. Pia, a woman with no children of her own, had shown him that. And soon they'd witness parenthood's most wondrous miracle together.

He wondered if being present as a new child entered the world would affect her emotions as it had his. Or if sharing such an intimate event would draw them closer.

He pocketed his wallet and strode toward Jennifer's rooms, an uncharacteristic bounce in his step.

As long as Pia stayed at the hospital, he'd stay.

PIA FORCED herself to keep calm as she pulled Jennifer's hospital room door closed behind her, then made her way toward the coffee machine, which was located near the nurses' station and across from the maternity ward's waiting room. She needed a double, and fast. As unsettling as reading the pregnancy manual had been, watching her friend ride through wave after wave of contractions made the pages of the pregnancy book seem as serious as a morning cartoon in comparison. As with everything in her life, Jennifer faced the onset of labor with quiet courage. Pia, however, felt agitation creeping up at her inability to do anything but offer comforting words. She'd hidden her frustration from Jennifer, but a mega shot of caffeine would help tamp it down.

"How is she doing?"

Pia's head snapped up at the sound of Federico's voice, which was entirely too smooth and cultured for six-thirty in the morning. "You're still here?"

Federico smiled, stretching his long legs out from under one of the narrow chairs lining the maternity ward's waiting room, just steps down the hall from Jennifer's room. He had the entire space to himself. "I talked to my father about a half hour ago. Antony is due to land shortly, and I wanted to stay until he arrived, at least." He stood, looking her over. Tentatively, he moved forward and put a hand on her shoulder. "I know I asked how Jennifer fared, but I should have asked about you. You look...unwell."

"You can say it. I look like hell."

His eyes crinkled with amusement. "No, not so bad as that. Besides, I don't believe I am permitted to say someone looks like hell. Quite a breach of etiquette for a prince."

"You used a contraction, though. You just said 'don't.' Even if you do fixate on proper manners, you're learning to loosen up a little."

His smile turned to a full-fledged grin, one that made his eyes sparkle despite the early hour. "You see? Spending time with you makes me a better person. Stay a few weeks longer and I should be able to pass as an American next time I visit the States."

"Now you're getting ambitious," she teased, unwilling to think about the seriousness of the invitation—or lack thereof. "Walk with me to the coffee machine? I really need my fix."

"I would like a cup myself."

Once he'd fallen into step beside her, she said, "I've been around pregnant women before, but it was always as part of the staff at a refugee camp, sorting out the emergency cases from nonemergency, and arranging for the pregnant women to receive medical care. It's different attending a birth in person, especially when it's your friend." She knew her fear was evident in her voice, but tried to cover it by looking at an infant CPR poster adorning one of the walls. "I'm used to seeing people in pain. But when it's Jen who's in pain and there's nothing I can do about it, and it's taking so long—" She released a long breath. "I'm sorry. I guess I'm tired from being up all night. My frustration is showing."

She flexed her fingers in an attempt to calm herself, then met Federico's worried look. "In answer to your original question, she's doing as well as can be expected with a first baby. I ducked out to give the anesthesiologist room to work while he gives her an epidural. I'm sure once that's done, she'll feel better. She wanted to wait as long as possible to get one and skip it if she thought she could. She finally said she couldn't."

Pia knew her words came out too fast, betraying her nerves despite her efforts to settle them. Without a word, Federico pulled her into his arms. Into her hair, he said, "It is exciting and frightening and overwhelming all at once."

"That's exactly what it is."

Her arms went around his waist, as naturally as if they held each other all the time. He took a deep breath, allowing his chest to rise and fall against hers. "Being present at the birth of a child forces you to reevaluate your priorities. To see what is important in life."

She smiled to herself, happy for his offer of reassurance after a long night without sleep, yet wary of what his protective embrace and tender words did to her emotions.

"How do women do this every day?" she mumbled against his chest.

"They don't do it every day. Just once or twice in a lifetime." A soft laugh rumbled through his rib cage. "Or in my mother's case, four times."

"I doubt I could do it once. Being with Jennifer is enough."

He drew one hand along her back, his warm touch both a relief and a danger to her. "Sometimes, I think watching is worse than having the baby yourself. I was with Lucrezia when she gave birth to each of our sons. The first time, I got lightheaded and feared I might lose consciousness. One of the nurses had to bring me water. Of course, Lucrezia barely seemed to break a sweat."

She tipped her head back to study his face. "You can't be serious. You nearly fainted? *You?*"

"Yes. They even brought me one of those...I think you call it a basin? The blue plastic bin for someone to be sick." The slightest blush touched his high cheekbones, and his grin turned sheepish. "I told you, I am no Prince Perfect. If I were, I would have stood by her side the whole time and held her hand without feeling anything but pride in her. Fortunately, the hospital staff signed a confidentiality agreement with our family, so my sickness never made the papers."

"I expect you were better with Paolo."

"I was. You will be fine with Jennifer, too." He held her tighter, and she couldn't help but notice how easily her head tucked under his chin, how well her arms fit around his lean waist. All too soon, he let her go, and a moment later she realized that Jennifer's labor and delivery nurse was approaching to indicate that she could come back inside. Federico must have heard her coming.

"Would you like me to bring you a coffee?" Federico asked.

"Princes do that?"

"When a woman stands in for that prince's absent brother, yes."

She grinned. "In that case, I'd love a double. I take it—"

"Skimmed milk, no sugar?"

Pia's mouth opened in surprise, and his mouth curled into a self-satisfied smile. "I noticed at breakfast yesterday. I prefer mine the same."

Ten minutes later, however, it was Antony who carried the steaming cup of coffee into Jennifer's room. He passed it to Pia with a quick word of gratitude, though his attention was riveted on his laboring wife.

"Why don't I leave you two alone?" she whispered to the crown prince.

He cast a distracted look her way and nodded. "Thank you."

Jennifer, who lay on her side, clearly uncomfortable, but better for having the pain-blocking epidural, mumbled her thanks. Pia gave her some words of encouragement, then strode back into the hall. Other than a nurse who was walking toward Jennifer's room, she encountered no one until she reached Federico in the waiting room.

"I see you have your coffee," Federico sipped from his own cup as he strode back and forth in front of the CPR poster.

"Nice delivery service. It's not every day a woman has two princes bring her caffeine supply." She exhaled, amazed at how Federico both calmed her fears and sent her body into overdrive with nothing more than a look.

The prince stopped pacing and tilted his head toward the room. "Any idea how much longer?"

"I'm guessing two more hours. Maybe three."

They both glanced at the oversize black-and-white clock suspended from the hallway ceiling, where the long hand shifted to click off another minute. "I have not yet purchased a gift for the baby. Perhaps we can make a quick visit to the gift shop? It should open soon."

Pia nodded her agreement and gestured for Federico to lead the way. They left the maternity ward and entered the waiting elevator, each acutely aware of each other's presence in the confined space. Seconds later, the lift stopped on the floor below to admit a tired girl in a wheelchair. One leg was elevated in front of her and bore a heavy cast that appeared new. The nurse pushing the chair hesitated at seeing the prince, but he gestured for her to enter and held the door open until the child was safely inside.

"You're Prince Federico!" Excitement laced the girl's voice as she realized who stood before her.

Crouching down, he replied, "I am. What is your name?"

"Carlotta."

He angled a look at her cast. "It looks like you broke your leg, Carlotta."

"Two places. I fell off the balance beam at gymnastics and had surgery yesterday to fix it. I have to wear this for two weeks before they take it off and give me a different kind."

He directed his gaze toward her arms, which stuck out of the sleeves of the hospital gown. She had a good deal of muscle, particularly for someone her age.

"You must train hard. That will help you recover quickly."

The doors closed, and after the nurse punched the appropriate button, Federico leaned forward to whisper to Carlotta in a voice just loud enough for Pia and the nurse to hear, "Are you going to leave your cast clean, or have your friends sign it? Is that still done?"

She nodded. "One of my friends said she'd do a sketch. She's a fantastic artist. Everyone else will probably just sign it."

Federico considered this. "You'd probably prefer your friends to sign it first, but may I?"

"Would you? Really?"

"I would be honored." The nurse handed Federico a pen from her lapel pocket, and he signed the cast in quick, fluid strokes. The doors opened on the girl's floor, and Federico returned the pen to the nurse with a smile of thanks before returning his focus to the gymnast. "Get well soon, Carlotta."

"I will!"

The nurse wheeled her charge out of the elevator, then both nurse and patient looked back and waved before the doors slid closed again.

Federico turned to Pia and started to say something, but closed his mouth and reached toward the corner of her eye. "What is this about?"

Pia blinked in shock, realizing that he'd wiped away a tear. She almost told him she had dirt in her eye, but he'd know it for a lie. "You must think I'm the world's biggest wimp."

Genuine puzzlement crossed his face. "Why would you say that?"

"Well, first, I'm barely holding it together in there for Jennifer. Then I nearly lost it yesterday when Paolo made his little fountain joke. And that girl...the way you made her day was so sweet. You talked to her as if she were your peer." Embarrassment caused her cheeks to heat. "I'm not this way all the time, really."

"I doubt you could work with refugees, or those dealing with HIV, if you did not possess a great deal of fortitude and the ability to talk to those in pain without talking down to them."

"It's just kids." She knew she was babbling but couldn't stop. "I've never been very good with them, and when I see them hurting, like that girl—"

"Now you are the one joking, right?"

"I'm afraid not."

"But you have been wonderful with Arturo and Paolo." His features softened, and Pia marveled at how Federico's love of his sons radiated from him as he spoke. "Not only yesterday, in the garden, but when they hit you with the boomerang. Many adults would have lost their temper, or at least given the boys nasty looks. You went out of your way to make them feel better about themselves. You realized how upset they were and made an effort to comfort them even though you were the one bleeding."

They exited the elevator and turned left, following the signs that pointed them toward the gift shop. They spotted its glass door ahead, but the lights remained off and a closed sign on the door. They slowed their pace, and he picked up the conversation. "You have a natural skill with children. And with adults, as well. The nurse who came out of Jennifer's room a few hours ago told me that Jennifer was holding up better than expected for her first labor and delivery, since she had you to keep her company. You were rubbing her back, helping with her breathing…I don't think you give yourself enough credit."

He paused, waiting for her to meet his gaze. When she did, the intensity of his blue eyes and his serious expression rendered her motionless.

"Federico?"

"I wanted to tell you" —he inhaled sharply— "I was wrong yesterday. When I made that comment as we left the garden with Paolo and Arturo. I owe you an apology."

That confused her. "What comment?"

"That you would make a good wife and mother for someone."

She did a double take, then continued walking, hoping he didn't notice her reaction. "You're apologizing for that? It was a nice compliment. Unless, of course, you didn't mean it."

"No." He touched her shoulder, stopping her. "It was wrong for me to say that after what happened the last time we were here, in the hospital. After I kissed you. What I really thought was that you would make a wonderful wife for me and mother to my children, even though it would have been completely inappropriate to say it."

Pia fought not to show her shock at his words. He continued, "It felt so easy, playing in the rain with the boys." He swiped a hand over his head, as if struggling for the correct words. "I have never felt that relaxed before. So comfortable with a woman, and with my children. Yet it was not simply *comfortable*. There was something more. I could not help but wonder if we...."

Pia clenched her coffee cup tighter to steady her hands. Federico diTalora, the man every woman in the Western world wanted, found "something more" with her? A woman who couldn't tell Prada from Chanel even on pain of death?

Impossible. Still, she had to know, had to hear him speak the words. "We—?"

"If there was the potential for a relationship." Emotion colored his speech, and for the first time since meeting him, Pia wondered if Federico experienced nervousness. "I was sincere when I said that I must honor Lucrezia. She was my dearest friend. But if I were ever to date or marry again, well...I hope it would be with a woman like you."

He reached out and touched her hand, his fingers moving over hers. Though his touch was gentle, no one who noticed them standing near the doors to the hospital gift shop would mistake the connection for anything but a romantic one. "How does a man who has two small children, and who lives his whole life before cameras, ask a woman if she might consider spending time with him?"

Pia could do nothing more than stare at the prince, riveted by his words, by the mixture of hope and fear in his voice, and by the bare desire in his gaze. Words refused to pass her lips, but she knew her answer was written all over her face.

He only needed to ask.

Thankfully, Federico relieved Pia of the need to speak by tossing his empty coffee cup into a nearby garbage can and pulling her slowly away from the gift shop. Hand in hand, they made their way along the hall in silence, desperate to escape the curious stares of patients, visitors, and staff who would occupy the halls as the sun rose and a new shift arrived. He guided her to a stairwell, up one flight, then along a series of short corridors. Without warning, he pulled her into a darkened office, shut the door behind them, and flipped the deadbolt.

"This belongs to our family doctor." Federico's voice came out barely above a whisper. He took Pia's coffee cup from her free hand and reached past her, brushing his upper body against hers, to set it on the desk. "I shall have to remind him to keep it locked."

"He came to the hospital earlier to inquire about Jennifer," Pia managed, though having her fingers still intertwined with Federico's muddied her thoughts. There was only one reason he'd bring her in here.

She turned her head to study the room. The fluorescent lights of the hallway filtered through the door's smoky glass, casting the room in a diffused light. Patient files filled a tray on one side of the desk, but otherwise the room was clean and neat. She took a half step back from him. As much as her body sensed the inevitable, and craved it, her brain continued to fight. "If he left it unlocked, it probably means he'll be back."

"He left the maternity ward an hour ago. His car keys were in his hand." Federico cupped Pia's chin and turned her head so her mouth met his.

Doubt and desire warred within her in the heartbeat before his soft lips brushed hers, so gently as to afford her the opportunity to move away and end it right there, if she wished.

She realized that for the first time since they met, they were in a spot where no one would interrupt them. No kids, no photographers, no palace staff. It was only the two of them. He smelled wonderful. There was a solidity and a kindness to him that—when combined with the way he held her—proved irresistible.

She wanted him. Badly. In the space of a breath, she leaned into him and returned his kiss. He pulled her body hard against his, dashing any ability she had to protest, to tell him that she'd already received the call to leave San Rimini, and that long before she'd even met him, she'd learned she'd never be the right fit for a man like him.

A low sound came from the back of his throat. At her core, something unfurled. Her fingers went to his waist, then slowly moved upward.

What was the harm in a kiss, really? She knew she'd never get him out of her system. Since that first stolen kiss, he'd filled her every waking thought. Nothing too intense could happen in a public hospital, so why not grab one more memory? It'd give her something to dream about the next time she found herself working to set up a food line in a crowded camp, or standing inside a stifling hut, talking to women about AIDS prevention.

She opened her mouth to his, tasting a hint of coffee as he slowly eased her toward the desk. In the nick of time, she broke the kiss long enough to move the coffee cup he'd left near its edge. Then, running her hands in slow, worshipful patterns across his broad chest and arms, she discovered firm, perfectly proportioned muscle beneath her fingertips. Despite his tightly regimented life, Federico obviously found time for exercise—lots of it, judging from the way his shoulders strained the cotton of his gray polo shirt. While the man looked incredible in a suit, it hid a lot of that hard work.

He smiled against her mouth, knowing exactly what she was doing.

Between kisses, she murmured, "This is so unfair. When could you possibly—?"

"Five in the morning," he whispered, reading her mind. "Before the boys are awake. It is the only time I have completely to myself."

How much was there to discover about him? And how much would she regret it when she left for her work in Africa? It had to be done. She'd made the commitment, and hundreds of people counted on her.

He bent to capture her lips again, teasing, pulling, nipping. He shifted to tease the tender spot where her jaw met her ear, then drifted downward, kissing the column of her throat with a heat that left her mind reeling. He lifted her onto the desk, and without thinking, she wrapped her legs around his waist and her arms around his shoulders, planting one palm against his nape to hold him to her. What would she do to have this man naked in her bed?

And how amazing would it be?, a dangerous part of her mind contemplated.

His hands tangled in her hair, and their kisses grew more heated, and more romantic. When he raised his head, glazed, sultry eyes met hers. He leaned in to take her mouth once more, but hesitated, moving to plant a lingering kiss against her cheek instead, before turning to whisper in her ear.

"I hope this means you will consider staying."

CHAPTER 8

FEDERICO PULLED BACK when she didn't answer. He didn't like the note of wariness in her eyes. "For a while," he clarified. "And not as a nanny to my sons. For us. There is something unique between us, and I would like to see where it leads."

Unless she didn't want to, he almost added. Had he moved too quickly? He'd never dated in the traditional sense. Even before Lucrezia, most of those dates were arranged, set up either by friends in their social set or by his parents. Perhaps, overcome by the sense of optimism Pia had stirred in him, he'd gone about it incorrectly.

"I can't." Her eyes clouded and her expression became unreadable. "But it's not you, Federico. It's me."

He dropped his hands from her and forced a smile, though he knew it didn't reach his eyes. "I have seen enough American television to understand that is what you call a 'polite brush-off,' yes?"

"No, no. It's just...my supervisor called last night from D.C. I can't stay. I'm scheduled to begin my next assignment a week from today."

"If you wished to stay, could you postpone it?" She opened her mouth, but at her uncomfortable expression, he responded for her. "But you do not wish to stay. I understand, and I was wrong to ask. It is who you are."

He turned toward the door, but her touch on his arm stopped him.

"I'm sorry, Federico." Her eyes brightened, but she blinked back the tears before they fell. "I want to give this a try, more than you know, but in the long run, I'd do you a disservice by staying."

So she did have feelings for him.

He released a long breath, then turned to sit on the desktop beside her. Lucrezia. It had to be Lucrezia.

He wasn't the type to discuss his personal life with others. Not only was he reserved by nature, indiscretion posed a great risk to someone of his birthright. However, if he didn't explain himself, he might never find the happiness that Antony, Marco, or Isabella had in their lives.

In taking Lucrezia from him—as painful as it was—fate had afforded him a second chance. He couldn't let it pass. He wasn't sure he could explain that without sounding heartless, but there was something companionable about sitting beside Pia, shoulder to shoulder, that made him realize his best option was to tell her everything and hope for the best.

"Pia, there is something I must explain." He braced himself, then continued, "I allowed you to believe an untruth about me when I picked you up at the airport, the day you arrived in San Rimini."

She frowned. "What?"

"I did not wish for them to marry." At her look of confusion, he added, "Antony and Jennifer, I mean. When Antony first pursued Jennifer, I told him I did not believe it was wise, and that they should not marry."

Pia raised her hip on the desk and angled her head to stare at him. He could tell she remembered their conversation in the limousine, when she'd made an offhanded comment about how she couldn't believe that Jennifer and Antony were married, let alone about to become parents.

"Why not?"

"I felt that a prince—a crown prince, in particular—should marry someone of stature, of an aristocratic family. Someone who understood our country and its traditions, someone who understood the breadth and depth of the role Antony was destined to fulfill as a future king. I did not believe an untitled woman—an American, and a relief worker—could possibly do that, despite the fact I had met Jennifer and admired her. And despite the fact I knew Antony had, well—"

"Fallen in love?" she asked softly.

He nodded. "It was obvious the first time I met Jennifer at a palace function how Antony felt about her. His eyes never left her. She made him reconsider his goals and his desires. She treated him as a man and as a peer, not a prince. And he loved her for it. He loved how it made him feel when he could reciprocate and challenge her to be a better person. They formed a bond. A tight one."

Pia seemed to wrestle with the information. Her hazel eyes focused on his jaw for several seconds before she lifted her chin to meet his gaze. "Why are you telling me this?"

"Because I was mistaken in my assessment. Antony could not have found a better bride, a better mother for his children, or a better woman to someday become San Rimini's queen." Federico glanced toward the door. Somewhere, several floors away, Antony and Jennifer were about to become parents. Their love for each other would only grow as their family grew, unlike what happened in his own marriage. Nothing had changed between him and Lucrezia. They started as friends and finished as friends.

"If I was mistaken about Jennifer, perhaps I was mistaken in other things." Pia had one hand on her thigh, and he reached to caress her knuckles. "It is not something I wish to admit, but I was mistaken to marry Lucrezia. I knew it in my heart during our marriage, but I ignored it. It was easy to go through my routine each day and focus on the friendship we shared, and on our boys. There was no strife, no conflict. But on the day Lucrezia died, when I learned that Marco was going to forgo his relationship with Amanda and follow my father's suggestion of pursuing an arranged marriage, I realized how wrong I was to have married her."

"Marco wanted to—?"

He waved off her confused look. "It is a long story. My point is that when Lucrezia died, I realized that I had robbed her of the chance to live her life with someone who truly loved her. She should have been married to someone who was more than her friend and confidant. She should have had all that and passion. A husband who woke up in the morning thinking of her, and who returned to her each night with anticipation. I went into mourning for her, but I also went into mourning for what she should have had. She did not have the opportunity to live her life to the fullest, and that was my fault. I told Marco not to make the same mistake I had made. I told him he needed to explore what he had with Amanda."

Pia remained quiet. He gave her hand a gentle squeeze and said, "It wasn't until yesterday, when we spent the afternoon playing in the garden, that I finally understood that marrying Lucrezia was a mistake for me, as well. I robbed myself of an opportunity, I did not simply rob Lucrezia of one."

"You married her, but you didn't love her?" Pia's voice cracked on the last few words.

"I loved her, but I was not *in* love with her. Lucrezia was a dear friend, someone I had known and understood since childhood. I married her because it was good for San Rimini, because I understood from birth that I must marry well, and that I must produce heirs so the diTalora family would remain on the throne and our nation would remain politically stable. It is what every generation did before mine. Who was I to act differently?"

At the look of doubt on Pia's face, he added, "Do not mistake me. Lucrezia and I got along well. I respected her, and I miss her every day. But there was no passion in our marriage."

They sat in silence for a long moment. When Pia finally spoke, her words were measured. "Would you do it over again, though? Duty is important to you. Not to mention your family and your nation."

He eased off the desk and turned to face her. He needed to drive home the importance of his words. "No, and not only because I was wrong to cheat Lucrezia out of the life she deserved. Because I followed my duty and ignored my own heart, I missed the opportunity to marry someone like you. Someone who speaks to me as if I

were any other human being and not a prince. Someone who appreci-
ates my children, and whom they appreciate in return. A woman who
cares for her friends when they need her, who can handle any crisis,
and who cares about those who cannot help themselves. Someone
who makes me want to sneak into a closed office so I can hold her and
kiss her because I do not wish to wait another moment to do so. I
cheated myself out of what Antony and Jennifer share." He captured
her face between his hands. "Pia, we could share such a love. A
passionate love. I feel a connection to you and a pull I have never felt
with another woman, and I am confident enough in it to know you
feel that, too. But it will not happen if you leave and we deny
ourselves the opportunity to get to know each other better and
discover it."

He slid his hands down her shoulders until he held her hands once
more. He marveled at how many lives she'd improved. How many
times, he wondered, had Pia's hands directed a frightened, exhausted
person to shelter for the night or served food to the hungry?

How could he have ever thought her scruffy and brash when she
was closer to perfect than he'd ever be?

"I believe," he met her gaze again, "that you are even more bound
to duty than I. This is why you choose to go to Africa, rather than
pursuing your heart's desire. By following your duty, you could make
the same mistake I once made. Do you not think so?"

To his shock, she shook her head. He'd expected a few moments'
consideration, then a "perhaps you're right." Instead, her jaw tightened
and she refused to meet his gaze.

"I think," she finally whispered, "they call you Prince Perfect
because you see the goodness in others, even when it isn't there."

She slipped her hands from his, touched her index finger to her
lips, and then to his. Pain filled her eyes at the contact. "I'm not that
noble, Federico. I'm going to Africa because I'm not strong enough to
stay here." She slid off the desk and eased past him, then flipped the
deadbolt on the office door. She started to turn the knob, then paused.
"Why don't you go to the gift shop? I'll meet you in Jen's room. She'll
want me there when the baby arrives. Then we can go our separate

ways and do what's best in the long run. What we shared here can stay here."

With that, she turned the knob and strode toward the elevators.

PIA COLLAPSED against the cold metal wall of the elevator the instant its doors closed, hiding her from the world. Using the flat of her hand, she blotted her tears then dried her hands on her slacks. Why did Federico have to be so damned *perfect*?

How could she be so *not*?

She was a chicken. A big, cowardly, confused chicken.

She'd allowed herself to kiss him because she'd convinced herself he could never be serious about her. A man still in mourning for his beloved wife was nothing more than a man on the rebound, one who'd forget her before her plane was wheels up.

But apparently, Federico wasn't a man on the rebound. He was a man experiencing true attraction for—quite possibly—the first time. As much as that idea flattered her, if she stayed, knowing that she could never truly give herself to him, then she was treating him no better than he'd treated Lucrezia.

Worse, even.

Pia swallowed a fresh bubble of sorrow before it broke to the surface. Jennifer needed her now. Before facing her friend—or holding Jennifer's child—she had to forget everything Federico told her. The last thing she needed was to lose her concentration when an infant, especially one so tiny, rested in her clumsy arms.

She might be falling for Prince Federico—no, she *knew* she was falling for him, had known long before he'd pulled her into the office to kiss her, and before he told her the truth about his marriage—but her own demons were stronger. More dangerous. If she succumbed to temptation and pretended to Federico and to herself that she could be everything he wanted her to be, he and his children would be hurt. Maybe not tomorrow, or the next day, but eventually.

How could she do that when hundreds of other women—women

who'd who make far better mothers to Arturo and Paolo—would love Federico for all he was, and would marry him in a heartbeat?

And she had no illusions about the fact he was the traditional, marrying type. He would marry again, this time for love.

As she left the elevator on the maternity level, the sound of happy cheers reached her ears. Within seconds, she turned the corner near the waiting room to see clusters of blue balloons tied to the nursing station, compliments of the medical staff, who'd apparently had them hidden away awaiting the royal infant's arrival. Curious doctors and nurses filled the hall, smiling and hugging.

Jennifer had sailed through the end of her labor and delivered a healthy baby boy. A future king.

When Pia managed to make her way through the celebratory staffers and reached Jennifer's door, a genuine smile lit her face at the scene inside.

It boggled the mind that one's demons could be so incredibly cute.

***

FEDERICO HALTED outside the door to Jennifer's room at the sight of his sister-in-law slumbering. Beside her, on an uncomfortable-looking chair, Antony shifted, half asleep, his head braced on one fist, his elbow propped on the arm of the chair. Federico took a cautious step inside, hoping to see Pia and lure her out, but the room was empty save the new parents.

Federico turned to leave but stopped at the sound of Antony gently clearing his throat, hoping to catch his attention without waking Jennifer.

"All well?" Federico mouthed.

Antony nodded, straightening in the chair and gesturing Federico back inside. In a whisper, the crown prince explained, "My son is across the hall, in the nursery. He just had his first bath."

Federico grinned at the pride in his older brother's voice. "And he is as tired as his mother, yes?"

Antony nodded. "It has been a long day for all of us. I have not checked on him for an hour or so. Would you mind—"

"Of course. You rest. You will not have the opportunity once you return to La Rocca." He cocked his head toward the window. Several stories below, a cadre of reporters from around the world waited for the chance to photograph the new family and ask questions. "Not only with them, but with the talks in the Middle East."

"I am all too aware. If anything is amiss, wake me?"

Federico nodded. Antony took a deep breath and put a hand on the bed beside his sleeping wife, then leaned back in his chair and closed his eyes, savoring his first hours as a parent.

Federico backed out of the room, fighting back the wave of jealousy that washed over him.

He could easily envision having the same life with Pia, given some time. Lying next to her, their heads side by side on their pillows after the boys were asleep, discussing what adventures the next day might hold. Finger combing her wild blond hair away from her face to look into her soft hazel eyes and kiss her goodnight, or to awaken her in the morning. Watching over her as Antony did Jennifer.

He gave himself a mental shake as he strode toward the nursery. His fantasies were light years ahead of rational thought. Anyone who felt this way about another human being so soon after meeting them had to be infatuated.

On the other hand, he'd spent enough years in emotional solitude to know he wasn't just anyone.

He met women day in and day out. Talked to them, made friends with them, worked on projects with them. No one had stirred him the way Pia Renati had.

Not only did he find her physically beautiful, despite the fact her wild hair and casual style were one hundred and eighty degrees from the women who tended to frequent his life, but Pia, when she relaxed, showed a sharp wit, a big heart, and an intellect that would fascinate him every day of his life.

Part of him thought he'd be an idiot to invite a woman into his life after the disaster he'd created by marrying Lucrezia, but the bigger part of him wanted Pia. Desperately. Public opinion didn't matter. Duty didn't matter.

He mattered. His sons mattered.

Pia mattered.

He swore under his breath in frustration. No woman had ever looked at him as she had, or kissed him as she did, with such intensity.

So what was it that made her afraid?

When he'd returned to Jennifer's room from the gift shop with a large stuffed bear in one hand and a bouquet of flowers in the other, Pia drew his attention before could take in the room. A look of panic had flashed across her face, then disappeared. In the instant he read her expression, he realized that Jennifer had already given birth and that he'd walked right past all the balloons at the nurses' station without absorbing why they were there. Antony had waved him inside, and soon he was distracted by the bundle in Jennifer's arms. But he wasn't so distracted that Pia's presence—and then her sudden disappearance—hadn't registered. He didn't think Pia even had the chance to hold the baby, with all the medical staff drifting in and out of the room at the time. The disappointment he felt knowing that she'd not only rejected his suggestion, but that she didn't wish to remain in the same room with him, caused a physical ache in his chest.

He wished he understood it.

He approached the nurses' station, where he was escorted into the nursery with a warning to keep quiet. At the exact moment it occurred to him that Pia might have come here, he saw her leaning over the new prince's bassinet.

Her back was to him, but the nurse beside Pia, more accustomed to the comings and goings of the maternity ward, noted his entrance. Unwilling to disturb Pia, he sliced his hand through the air, warning the nurse not to say anything. The nurse blinked her understanding, then focused on Pia. Speaking in San Riminian-accented Italian, she said, "You may hold him, if you wish. The parents have given their permission."

"Oh, no," Pia whispered, her own Italian soft and melodic, but her nervousness at such a proposition clear from her stiffening spine. "He looks happy where he is."

The brunette nurse gave Pia a soft smile. "It will be practice for the christening. I was told that you will be the godmother. And new babies like to be held." The nurse gestured toward the end of a row of bassinets, several of which were occupied by sleeping infants. "Take a seat in the rocking chair. I'll give him to you."

Pia hesitated, then moved to the end of the row and sat, her back still to Federico. "I'm not very good with children."

The nurse tightened the blanket around the wide-eyed baby boy, then placed the burrito-like bundle into Pia's arms. "Not to worry. I know he will like you."

"It's not that." Apprehension colored Pia's voice as she stared down at the little boy in wonder. "I tend to break them."

The nurse sat on the footrest in front of Pia's rocker. "Not under my observation, you won't. You are doing fine. See, he is trying to get his arm free, to reach for your finger."

Federico watched a moment longer, as the nurse continued to speak softly to Pia and the baby. Pia gradually sank back against the wooden slats of her rocking chair.

"The pregnancy and parenting books make it all look so easy," he heard Pia say.

"And the weight loss commercials make it look like anyone can knock off ten kilos without exercising or craving cannoli," the nurse deadpanned. "It all takes practice. You'll get there. The baby won't break."

Pia let out a ragged breath but didn't respond.

Without a word, Federico eased out of the nursery.

CHAPTER 9

"Your Highness, your first interview is in half an hour. The christening is at eleven, followed by the luncheon, then I have the remaining three candidates scheduled for late afternoon. Would you care to review their résumés?"

Federico looked up from his desk, where a large stack of correspondence awaited his perusal, to see Teodora entering his office. He'd been daydreaming again—a luxury he rarely afforded himself—but he couldn't eradicate thoughts of what he and Pia had shared in the hospital, and what he'd witnessed in the nursery.

A week had elapsed since then, but all time had done was make him think about her more. Even burying himself in work and the hunt for a new nanny hadn't distracted him.

Of course, it hadn't helped that they'd spent the bulk of that week together, albeit under the eyes of others. Now that Isabella and Marco were back at La Rocca with their respective spouses, the family dining room had become the center of action, with everyone lingering over meals, given that they'd all arranged for lighter work schedules for the days between the birth and the christening. Pia had been a fixture at those gatherings, staying after dinner to play cards with his siblings, engage in hotly debated games of checkers with Paolo, and to teach

Arturo chess. When the family wasn't congregated in the dining room, the glorious early autumn weather had drawn the entire clan into the gardens. Pia had joined them on nearly every occasion, even pitching in to help when Marco suggested setting up a badminton net.

Each day, Federico grew more and more drawn to her. She had a positive outlook on life that he admired, she was patient with his boys, and she grew more comfortable with his siblings and their individual quirks with each passing day. She'd even called out Marco when she'd suspected him of cheating at cards, then gave everyone heartwarming updates on Jennifer's recovery until night before last, when Jennifer felt well enough to join everyone for dinner. Afterward, they'd all watched a Disney movie in the palace library when Eduardo surprised them by setting up a large screen.

Federico had been seated beside Pia for meals on several occasions and had been her badminton partner twice. When Paolo decided he wanted to sit in Pia's lap for the movie, Federico had taken the empty spot beside them on the sofa, ready to retrieve the boy should he become too heavy.

Over the course of the week, they'd laughed together, they'd talked local politics and cinema, and they'd shared in meaningless witty banter, particularly during one heated badminton game against Marco and Amanda. But they hadn't touched, hadn't discussed anything serious. And they hadn't had a single moment alone.

The togetherness without privacy drove Federico mad.

Federico accepted the short stack of résumés from Teodora and flipped through them, though he was already familiar with the contents. He and Teodora had each spent time on the phone with the head of the agency discussing the candidates and had limited the interviews to these four. Each offered possibilities, but the idea of facing the candidates today, trying to ascertain who would best care for Arturo and Paolo and what type of influence they'd have on the boys, exhausted him.

He stared at the top page, which contained information on the candidate he'd interview first. After today, his world would change. He'd have a new nanny, and Pia would be gone.

According to Antony, she was scheduled to fly to Botswana tonight, after the christening of little Prince Gianluca, whom Antony and Jennifer had started to call Luc. He wasn't ready for her to get on the plane. But neither could he stop it.

"Prince Federico? May I help you with something?"

Federico blinked, caught once again staring into space. "I apologize. I have been distracted."

Teodora raised an eyebrow. "If you'd prefer, I'd be happy to conduct the interviews to narrow down the field."

He shook his head. "No, we have narrowed it as much as possible already. I need to spend as much time with the candidates as I can before making a decision."

His assistant nodded and headed for the office door, but he stopped her as an idea occurred to him. "Teodora, when am I scheduled to complete the interviews today?"

"By six or six-thirty, depending on how much time you spend with the candidates. You'll be able to enjoy the evening with your sons, if you wish. Princess Isabella offered to take them while you conduct the interviews."

He tapped his pen against the desk for a moment. It would be unprofessional, bordering on rude, but time was of the essence. He had to take his shot.

"Is it too late to reschedule this evening's interviews for tomorrow? There is something else I need to do, and if it works out, I want the rest of the evening clear." He outlined his plan, then said, "So?"

Teodora's mouth opened fractionally before she recovered, nodding as if the request represented nothing out of the ordinary. "Certainly, Your Highness. I believe Jennifer has already made the transportation arrangements, however—"

"Good. Offer the candidates my apologies for the last-minute change. If any of them cannot make it tomorrow, I will reschedule at their convenience, and will cover any expenses they might incur due to the late notice. Then call Harriet to rearrange the transportation. But please, do not tell Ms. Renati. I would like to surprise her."

Or, more accurately, keep her from evading him. Before she left La Rocca for good, he would have one last chance to speak to Pia.

PIA SHIFTED her feet on the aged marble floor, listening without hearing as the priest told the gathered diTalora family members how Gianluca's birth constituted a blessing for both his parents and the country he'd someday lead.

Other than the quiet ministrations of the priest, not a sound could be heard in the Duomo. Even the dust motes of the ancient cathedral had stilled for the ceremony, seeming to hang motionless in the filtered light from the stained-glass windows. Though Gianluca now stood second in line behind his father to the longest-held throne in Europe, Jennifer and Antony managed to keep the press out of the service. Only the godparents and immediate family were present, making it the most intimate ceremony the royal family had shared in years.

As the priest's words echoed through the cathedral's cavernous gray arches, Pia kept her gaze riveted on the infant. Blissfully asleep in Jennifer's arms, the child wore the same two-hundred-year-old white lace christening gown his father once wore. It took every ounce of Pia's will to keep her attention off Prince Federico, who stood opposite her before the altar.

She should have known that Jennifer and Antony would ask him to be Gianluca's godfather. Antony was closer to Federico than anyone except his own wife. And that meant, for better or worse, Pia and Federico would be tied together for life, in at least one small way. Thank goodness there was no godparent rule stating that they had to spend time nurturing the infant together.

Pia inhaled slowly in an effort to exude calm and tried not to think about Federico's words to her as she had entered the Duomo that morning. Over the rumble of organ music, he'd complimented her on her soft pink dress and choice of heels—both borrowed, of course— and then he'd mentioned that Arturo and Paolo looked forward to eating with her at the palace luncheon planned for after the christening.

He had said that they would miss her when she left, though the way he'd leaned in close to tell her left no doubt that he was including himself in the word "they." Then he mentioned that he'd be sitting beside her at the luncheon. His rich baritone had made her toes curl inside her high-heeled shoes.

It didn't help matters that he looked stunning in his immaculate navy blue suit. The light blue shirt he'd worn with it made his eyes all the brighter.

It was incredibly distracting.

Pia raised her eyes to the stunning rose window above Federico's head. Part of her—the logical part—had hoped that he'd forget about her over the course of the week while he went about his royal duties, cared for his children, and conducted his search for a new nanny. But when Gianluca made his appearance into the world, the family cut back on their public appearances, rescheduling many for after the christening. That meant her hours prior to the christening were spent ensconced at La Rocca with the entire diTalora clan...including Federico. She and Federico been partnered twice for badminton games, but their conversation had been light. Thanks to the presence of others, she'd been able to leave a buffer between herself and Federico during most meals and evening card games, as conversation focused on Nick and Isabella's honeymoon, on Marco and Amanda's recent and upcoming engagements, and on the new baby. Even on the night when Eduardo had surprised them all by showing a Disney movie in the library and Federico had taken the seat beside her, she'd had Paolo in her lap, chattering away about the characters, and had been able to shield herself from him.

All the while, though, she'd been acutely aware of Federico's presence.

Twice in the last week she'd seen him on television. Once, at the reopening of a historic home in the heart of the city—soon to be occupied by the new American ambassador—and then during a news program where he'd answered a reporter's inquiry by stating that yes, he was scheduling interviews for nanny candidates, that he had no preference for a male or female nanny, and that he hoped whomever he hired would have a positive, lasting influence on his children.

He'd also responded to a rather pointed question about her, replying that yes, Pia Renati was a friend of Jennifer's, and that no, there was no romantic relationship between them. He added that he found such intimate questions inappropriate, and that while he was a public figure and understood that the media was curious, Pia was not a public figure, which made such personal questions doubly inappropriate. He concluded by telling the reporter—and the media at large—to expect him to ignore future inquiries about romantic interests.

Hearing Federico say the words "no romantic relationship" made the emotional part of her ache with emptiness. That part of her still fantasized about having him cradle her face and look at her with desire in his eyes.

Common sense, however, told her it was all for the best.

As the priest touched the infant's head with holy water, Pia smiled down at Gianluca, who looked so tiny and fragile in his gown, and reminded herself that she'd made the right choice. During the past few days she'd spent enough time watching Jennifer with the baby to start feeling more confident around little Gianluca herself, but not enough to care for him without Jennifer or Antony's presence. Despite her wish to help so they might get more sleep, Pia wasn't sure she'd ever be able to stay alone with an infant without being overcome by waves of panic or mental replays of her teenage accident.

She was far better off going where she could be useful, working to help prevent the spread of HIV in areas where it was rampant. She could make a real difference in the lives of hundreds of people.

Gianluca gurgled, which made Antony laugh. Behind Antony, Federico's face lit with a radiant smile. She snapped her attention back to the baby at the same moment she sensed Federico raising his head to share that smile with her. Leaving San Rimini might be the logical thing to do, but it cut so close to her heart that she couldn't look at him. Not in that moment.

Organ music played to conclude the ceremony, then King Eduardo moved forward to hug his son and daughter-in-law and thank the priest. That done, they quickly reviewed plans for returning to La Rocca for the celebratory luncheon. The streets outside the Duomo were packed with citizens who had turned out for the chance to glimpse the next generation of the diTalora family. Though it wasn't as large a crowd as had gathered for Jennifer and Antony's wedding, it was enough for the noise to carry through the Duomo's thick walls, and to require the placement of barriers along the nearby streets to control the foot traffic.

Pia edged away from Federico to stand behind King Eduardo. Before she could slip out to one of the waiting vehicles, the king himself stopped her, thanking her for staying with Jennifer during the final weeks of her pregnancy. Federico used the opportunity to approach, and once his father finished speaking, the prince cupped her elbow and propelled her down the main aisle, between the wide rows of pews.

The move was so unexpected, Pia's heart rate soared as if she'd just taken a leap from an airplane. "Federico, what's wrong? What are you—?"

"Nothing is wrong. Ride to La Rocca with me."

CHAPTER 10

Pia speared him with a sideways glance. "I thought the plan was for me to ride with Marco and Amanda, while you—"

"There is a new plan. My father will be riding with Jennifer, Antony, and the baby in the lead car. Isabella and Nick will ride with Marco and Amanda."

In that instant, Pia realized the plans had changed because Federico changed them. She tried to school her features to prevent her alarm from showing as Federico continued, "It was announced this morning that we are the godparents. It only makes sense that we ride back to the palace together, *si*?"

"Won't the press think something is up?" She didn't have to add *between the two of us*. Given the questions they'd fielded after she'd received stitches at the hospital, they didn't need more rumors.

"The boys will ride with us, of course. Nothing could be up with two children at our sides."

Pia gauged her chances of escape and decided she had little choice. The fact that Amanda, Marco, Isabella, and Nick were already departing through the Duomo's side door toward the row of limousines that waited to carry them back to the palace sealed it.

"All right. I'll ride with you and the boys." She looked around for

Paolo and Arturo. They'd been so well behaved during the service, sitting on a pew behind their aunts and uncles, she'd forgotten they'd come with the king after she'd arrived.

Federico spotted the boys first, huddled together near the side door, giggling, the jackets on their tiny suits unbuttoned, their shirts partially untucked. The prince walked up behind them, and Pia followed, noticing as she approached that the boys had something hidden in their hands. They jumped when they realized their father stood over them.

"Um, are we ready to go, Papa?" Arturo asked, cupping his hands behind his back.

"Yes. If you show me what you are hiding, first."

"We got hungry," Paolo explained, despite a dirty look from Arturo. "The priest said we could."

"Arturo?" Federico fixed his gaze on his elder son. Arturo let out a deep sigh, then produced a handful of miniature chocolate bars. "I know we're not supposed to, Papa, but the priest gave them to us and I don't like appetizers."

Federico extended his hand. He'd apparently explained to the boys that a cocktail hour with appetizers would precede the luncheon. "All right. You may each have one now. I will hold the rest for later."

Grudgingly, Arturo handed over his loot, and Federico tidied the boys' shirts and jackets before steering them out the door to the waiting limousine. Pia barely managed to keep her expression serious during the exchange. Her own stomach rumbled at the sight of the chocolate bars, so she doubted the boys could wait two hours past their normal lunchtime to be fed.

She remained in the doorway as Federico and the boys paused outside the Duomo to greet the crowd. Arturo and Paolo had learned the drill early. They smiled, they waved, they posed for photos. After a reasonable interval, Federico extended a hand to Paolo, who took it. It was the signal that they were going to proceed to the limo. Once they were close to the vehicle, Pia slipped out of the Duomo and walked to the limo. She kept her chin lowered, but a smile on her face. An appropriate look for the godmother following a christening, she hoped.

Thankfully the ride would only take a few minutes, then she'd be able to nibble on puff pastry or mini quiche while circulating amongst the members of parliament and the aristocracy gathered for the cele-bratory lunch. Though the christening itself was limited to family, the luncheon was a bigger event. She had dreaded it earlier, but now real-ized it gave her the opportunity to slip away from Federico.

The prince handed her into the limousine before sliding in beside her. The boys had already buckled themselves on the bench seat opposite, with Arturo facing Federico and Paolo in a booster seat facing Pia. The children hummed with excitement now that they were done with what they'd thought of as a long, boring service. Their energy was contagious, helped along by the celebratory atmosphere of the crowd and the glorious sunshine. It gave her the sense of being cocooned in magic, in a place where nothing could go wrong, and where she belonged.

Pia took a long, deep breath, and ignored the urge to slide closer to Federico, to reach out and put her hand on his knee, and to tell him that yes, she'd made a terrible mistake, and that she'd love to stay and see if they could make a relationship work. Instead, aware of eyes both inside and outside the vehicle, she leaned forward, smiled, and talked to the boys. Any observer would think her focus was on them, and not on the prince beside her.

Reality was quite different. She grinned at Arturo when he asked why Gianluca had worn "a fancy lace dress," but as Federico informed his son that it was a christening gown, and explained that both Arturo and Paolo had worn the same one for their christenings, her every nerve ending seemed attuned to him. She was acutely aware of his hips depressing the seat cushion alongside hers, of the space his shoulders occupied against the seat back, and of the familiar, enticing scent of him. She was even aware of the spread of his fingers, where they rested on his knee in her peripheral vision.

How could one man possess so much charisma? The very air in the limousine seemed charged with his presence. It was a good thing the luncheon would be hosted in the palace's expansive Imperial Ballroom, because she'd need every molecule of that space.

"I understand you are scheduled to leave for Africa tonight," Federico said as the driver started the engine and pulled away from the Duomo to follow the other family vehicles. "Botswana, is it?"

She nodded. "It's currently the heart of the crisis. We have a center there."

He encouraged the boys to open their candy, then lowered his voice. "I realize that this is not the time or place, but I must speak with you before you go. I saw you in the hospital nursery on the day Gianluca was born. I walked in behind you and left before you saw me. I know I should have announced my presence, but I did not wish to interrupt." He drew a deep breath, and the pause felt momentous.

Pia turned to face him, instantly realizing what he must have overheard. She'd never wanted him to know the depth of her fears, especially since he had allowed her to play with his own two children, but maybe it was for the best. Maybe now he'd understand why she needed to move on.

"Pia, why did you tell the nurse—"

As high a stake as she had in the prince's words, a sudden noise from Paolo made her turn her attention toward the little boy. He whacked his fist against the side of his booster seat, then in the direction of his brother's knee.

"Paolo?" she asked. "Paolo, are you all right?"

Paolo's face went crimson. First his cheeks, then from the top of his head down to his throat. He sputtered, attempting to cough but failing. Panicked, he fixed his gaze on her, soundlessly pleading for help.

"He's choking," she told Federico, even as she unbuckled her seat belt and knelt in front of the boy. She freed him from his booster seat, leaned him forward into her arms, and pounded him on the back a few times. The wrapper of his candy bar remained clutched in his hand.

Pia worked quickly, loosening Paolo's tie and unbuttoning the top of his shirt. She leaned him forward and tried once more to dislodge the candy.

Federico knelt on the limousine floor beside Pia.

"Paolo, oh no, Paolo." He leaned over the children's seat, catching the driver's eye in the mirror. "Pull over, immediately. Then call for an ambulance."

"Your Highness, if we pull over here, we would be mobbed," the driver tilted his head toward the crowd lining the side of the cobblestoned street. "And with the street blocked off, an ambulance will have difficulty getting through. I recommend we pass your father's car and get to the palace." Without waiting for Federico's agreement, he snatched up the cell phone mounted to the dash and called ahead, telling whoever answered to have the doctor waiting by the palace's front doors.

In the meantime, Pia grabbed Paolo around the waist, wedging him into her lap as best she could in the confined space between the seats. With Paolo no longer able to breathe, Pia had no intention of waiting until they arrived at the palace.

"Paolo," she instructed, fighting to keep her voice firm as she hoisted him so his head was just in front of hers. "I'm going to put my hands under your ribs, here." She made a double fist with her hands and found into the tiny space at the base of his rib cage. "Try to go limp against me, okay?"

The little boy kept fighting, his instincts sending him scurrying toward his father. Arturo cried out for his brother, terror lacing his voice. Understanding what Pia needed, Federico ignored Arturo and focused on Paolo, encouraging his frightened son to listen to Pia. For just a moment, Paolo met his father's eyes and his body relaxed. Pia thrust her hands up and in, then did it again.

C'mon, Paolo, c'mon. Paolo's utter silence and his darkening face sent fingers of dread through Pia. She forced back the vision of a little girl's hair sailing over her head as she went airborne, gave an internal prayer, and tried a third time to eject the candy from Paolo's throat.

A half-melted piece of chocolate shot out of the little boy's mouth, landed on his father's slacks, and slid down to the floor.

Paolo crumpled. He sucked in a lungful of air, paused, then made a wheezing sound before a cry ripped from his lungs.

At once, Federico enclosed both of them in a hug. "All right, Paolo. You will be all right now. *Tutto va bene.*"

Pia dropped her head down on top of Paolo's, relief flooding through her. What would she have done had Paolo been unable to cough up the candy? Would they have made it to the palace? How would Federico have handled such devastation?

"Let's not do that again. You scared me, Paolo," she whispered against his soft brown hair, cradling him to her.

"Me, too," Federico murmured.

"Me, too!" Arturo cried, launching himself from his seat and clutching at Federico's broad shoulders.

She pressed a kiss to the top of Paolo's head and told him everything was all right, and he mumbled an "okay" between ragged, crying breaths. But now that the immediate danger had passed, the fight-or-flight part of her that resisted getting any closer to Federico or his family emerged.

Sitting on the floor of the car, even as the driver lurched along the cobblestoned streets at a breakneck pace to return to the palace, felt entirely too good. Being hugged by Federico and the boys felt too...too *right.* As if she'd finally become part of the loving family she'd wanted so badly as a child.

"Let's get you back in your car seat," she told Paolo as the limousine rounded another corner, "before there's another accident."

Paolo nodded, his bright pink face still registering shock from the episode. Silently, he climbed back into his booster seat. Federico leaned past her to tell the driver all was well and it was safe to slow down. As Pia latched Paolo's safety belt and Arturo clambered back onto his own seat and buckled in, Federico's hand warmed her shoulder.

Very quietly, he said, "*Grazie mille,* Pia. I have never assisted a choking victim before, let alone my own son. I am not sure I could have—"

"I'm sure. You would have." Pia turned to grab her seat belt, and a glance out the window surprised her with a view of the palace's impressive facade. She clicked the buckle into place and said, "I've never done anything like that before, either. If you'd asked me five minutes ago, even with all the first aid training I receive for my job, I would never have claimed to be confident I could handle a real-life situation."

"You should be confident."

Federico's tone was pointed, a reminder that he'd overheard her nursery conversation. Glancing at Paolo, and seeing his color returning to normal, she conceded that Federico had a point. Perhaps she wasn't as incapable as she'd always feared herself to be where a small child was concerned.

They rolled to a stop at the palace's grand front entrance. The reporters and cameramen who'd been afforded exclusive access to the palace grounds for the christening of San Rimini's future king surged against the rope that held them back from the vehicle. All of them yelled the same questions through the car windows—why had the occupants of the limousine been spotted on the floor? Why had they raced ahead of the procession? Was there an emergency?

Federico allowed his driver to open the car door, assuring the reporters he'd answer their questions momentarily. He reached back to help Pia from the car, and at the wave of cameras being raised, she reflexively gripped Federico's hand tighter than appropriate.

Once Federico unbuckled the boys, he handed them off to his assistant and the palace doctor, who had emerged from the palace as their vehicle had approached. Federico spoke quickly in Teodora's ear, telling her what happened in the car and asking her to have the doctor check Paolo before she took the boys to the reception.

Once both boys had been safely escorted inside, Federico eased Pia toward the palace steps, then turned to respond to the reporters' questions.

As Pia stood on the lowest step, a feeling of déjà vu gripped her. The sea of reporters mirrored the scene at the hospital the evening she'd received her stitches. On the other hand, her emotions concerning Federico were both stronger and more confused than they were then, when he'd given her that first searing, knee-weakening kiss.

She was going to remember that kiss in the hospital corridor the rest of her life.

She'd also remember helping Paolo, and this moment, for the rest of her life.

Federico raised his hands to quiet the buzz of the crowd. "In answer to your questions, we had a slight scare in the car. Nothing to worry about. I allowed Paolo to have some candy as we drove back here from the Duomo, and he decided it might be interesting to see what would happen if he swallowed it whole."

A few of the reporters smiled in response to Federico's light-hearted tone, though by their expressions, none seemed ready to accept such a simple explanation. Federico quickly added, "Thanks to Ms. Renati, nothing serious happened. Paolo, as you saw when we arrived, is perfectly fine. A little choked up over his cousin's christening, perhaps, but fine."

Pia eased backward, toward the palace entry and away from the journalists as they fired off a barrage of follow-up questions. "What exactly did she do?"

"Is she qualified to treat a member of the royal family?"

"How serious was the incident? Could Paolo breathe?"

"Did she need to use the Heimlich maneuver, or did Paolo simply cough up the candy?"

"Was he—"

Federico tried to speak over the noise, assuring them that Paolo was never in any real danger, but before the reporters could push him for more detail, the vehicle carrying King Eduardo, Antony and Jennifer, and the newly christened infant pulled into the circular drive. The new arrival distracted a number of the reporters, all of whom had been sent to La Rocca with the sole mission of obtaining photographs of the new heir to the throne.

Federico directed the rest of the reporters toward the crown prince's car, and said the palace would issue more information about Paolo later, if it was appropriate to do so. He gave them a final reassurance that his son was perfectly fine before turning toward the palace.

"Follow me." Federico said, nudging Pia. She did, and within seconds they were through the palace doors and surrounded by staff who stood ready to assist the guests who were scheduled to arrive behind the motorcade from the Duomo.

Pia glanced at Federico as they walked along the wide entrance hall toward the Imperial Ballroom. "You handled that well. I was afraid their questions would delay the other cars and force lunch to be postponed. I'm starved."

Federico didn't respond. Instead, once they were out of sight of the staff, in the rotunda outside the Imperial Ballroom, he took her hand and eased her onto a large upholstered sofa. It stood beneath a floor-to-ceiling window that opened onto the palace gardens, and the sunshine bathed her in warmth.

Or maybe that was due to the fact Federico not only held her hand, he'd angled his body so his knees touched hers.

She somehow kept her voice calm as she asked, "What's wrong?"

"Nothing is wrong, but you are not getting away so easily. From me, or from the conversation we started in the car."

Pia glanced back down the hall. The rest of the royal family hadn't yet entered the palace. She had to assume the reporters would occupy them for some time. "Listen, Federico—"

"What is it about children that terrifies you? Why are you using it as an excuse to leave, when your gut and your heart tell you that we are meant to be together?"

Pia fought the urge to stand and run. Somehow, he'd progressed from "stay and give it a try" when they were at the hospital to "meant to be together," despite the fact they hadn't had a moment alone since Gianluca's birth. It was a massive leap.

She stole another look toward the entrance, then said, "For a man who's spent his whole life playing the part of the circumspect prince, you sure can be blunt when you want to be."

"Pia."

"Okay, okay." She worried her lip and tried not to think about the fact that he still had her hand trapped in his. "It's not that children terrify me, exactly. I don't think I should be in a position of responsibility for them, that's all. It's not Arturo and Paolo. It's all children. I've made some serious mistakes. Anyone you pursue a relationship with needs to be someone you can trust with your boys. I'm not that person."

"Do you mean the sort of person who's caring, intelligent, and loving?"

"Federico, please—"

"I have seen you caring for Jennifer. You took time away from your job to do so, a job I know you value as much as I do mine. And I have seen you with my sons." He tightened his left hand around hers and cupped her chin with his right, forcing her to look into his sharp blue eyes. "I dare you, right now, to deny that you are all those things. And to deny that a large part of you wants to see what a future might hold for us. Please stay. Or go, if that is what you truly want. But do not use your fears as an excuse."

Tears tightened her throat before welling up in her eyes. She'd enjoyed being around Paolo and Arturo, but the day they'd spent exploring the garden in the rain had scared her. Playing cards and watching movies wasn't the same as being in their lives long term. It wasn't dealing with scrapes and falls, with bullies and bad behavior. And in her heart, she knew she would have run the other way from that day in the rain if she hadn't been encouraged by Jennifer, and if she hadn't had the stupid idea that spending time with Federico would make her realize her attraction to him was fleeting.

She'd failed miserably on that count.

Federico's invitation to stay was tempting, even if she could set aside her commitment at work. She doubted any woman in her right mind would turn her back on such an amazing man as Federico diTalora. But Pia knew her fears were based on real experience. They weren't an imagined excuse.

The boys didn't deserve that. Federico didn't deserve it, either. In the long run, he deserved to be with a devoted, loving partner. Someone who was as comfortable with palace life as Lucrezia had been, but who appreciated each facet of Federico's layered, complex personality. Who loved him as he deserved to be loved.

Maybe Federico thought he could love her. But he didn't realize the difference between the woman he saw and the woman she knew herself to be. He didn't see the mistakes she was still working to overcome.

She gathered herself and forced her gaze to his. For a moment, she wavered, then said, "It's no excuse. Believe me, Federico, I wish it were that simple. Going to Africa is the right thing for me to do."

CHAPTER 11

"WHY DO YOU DOUBT YOURSELF? This is not simply about responsibility, or you would not have the job you do." His eyes were shrewd and assessing, but his voice held a note of concern. "Are you unable to conceive? Is this why you are uncomfortable with children?"

She shook her head, cutting off the inquiry. "No, that's not it. I mean, I don't know. It's not the type of thing you usually discover unless you're in the situation."

He massaged the back of her hand with his thumb and nodded. "I know that infertility can affect someone deeply, which is why I asked. If that is not the issue, what is it about children that disturbs you? In the hospital nursery, when Gianluca was born, I overheard you tell the nurse that you feared you might break him. I cannot imagine such a thing, yet your apprehension was obvious. You have a concrete reason. I wish to hear it."

His gentle expression showed so much love, so much worry, that she knew she had to tell him. Then she had to hope he'd understand why she had to go, no matter how strong his feelings for her might be —or hers for him.

She eased her hand from his and straightened. "You've probably figured out that I don't get along with my mother so well."

Surprise flickered in his eyes. It wasn't at all what he'd expected her to say. "I wondered, but did not wish to ask. You were not comfortable talking about her at breakfast last week, the day we took the boys out in the rain."

Pia nodded. "My mother's a great person, and now that I'm an adult, I'm finally beginning to appreciate her. But when I was young, she wasn't around much. She wasn't the kind of parent I could emulate. When I was sixteen, I couldn't stand her. That's about the same time I landed my very first job, babysitting for a neighbor. The little girl was about Arturo's age."

As if knowing what she'd say next, he leaned forward. "What happened?"

"Long story short, the girl fell backward out of a swing. I pushed her too high and she lost her seat. She broke her arm and damaged her kidneys from landing so hard. She had to have surgery."

Pia closed her eyes for a moment, wishing never to imagine the little girl's stricken, pained look again. Those moments they'd waited for the paramedics had been gut-wrenching and had seemed to stretch forever. When Pia opened her eyes to Federico's concerned expression, she explained, "I felt horrible, and it only got worse when I tried to describe what happened to the girl's father. The ambulance arrived a few minutes before he did. As soon as they loaded his daughter inside, he turned and yelled at me like you wouldn't believe. He was this huge guy, muscular and scary, at least to me, even though he'd never been anything but kind to me before that day. When I finished telling him everything, he said I couldn't be trusted, and that he never should have hired a babysitter whose own mother couldn't take care of her. He drove to the hospital and left me there to walk home."

Pia screwed up her mouth at Federico's sickened look. "I know, I know. Now that I'm older, it's obvious that I shouldn't have believed him. He was under a lot of stress, accidents happen, he didn't mean what he said and all that. But deep down, I believed him. I knew I pushed his daughter too high in the swing and that the accident truly was my fault. I also knew that what he said about my mother was true, and he wasn't the only one to say it."

Federico released a long breath. "And now you believe that you cannot stay with me because I have Arturo and Paolo. Do you truly believe you would harm them?"

Pia pulled her hand from his and pressed her fingers to the base of her eye sockets in an attempt to hold in her tears. Talking about what happened all those years ago shouldn't still be so hard, but it was. "I'd never harm them. Not knowingly. But I have a lot of doubts. Most people would tell me my doubts aren't rational, but I care so much about you, Federico. I think I might even be in love with you." She bit down on her lower lip, knowing it was idiotic to have said the words, yet she'd been unable to stop them. "Let's just say that my feelings are strong enough not to put your sons at risk. There are literally millions of women in the world who would fall over themselves to be with you —intelligent, beautiful women without my issues. Women who would love you, and who would love the boys. You deserve that."

To her amazement, Federico laughed. It wasn't loud, but the shape of the rotunda caused it to echo.

"Pia." He eased her fingers away from her face, then smiled and shook his head. "We have much in common. After my experience with Lucrezia, I questioned myself, likely in much the same way as your experience has made you question yourself. I was certain I could not date without hurting the other person. That I would mistake comfort for love, or that I might be even be incapable of love. You were certain you could never care for children, that you were incapable of keeping them from harm."

"You make us sound so pathetic," she sighed. "How could you possibly think that we'd be good together?"

"Because we are both working to overcome our doubts. When I met you" —he briefly pressed one hand to his chest— "I finally understood that the right person could not only make me feel intense emotion, but could make me a better father to my children. You are learning that you can care for children without something terrible coming to pass."

Sarcasm edged her laugh. "Right. And what happened to Paolo just now? That wasn't so terrible."

"It wasn't terrible because you were there to help. The fact he choked was not your fault. *I* was the one who permitted him to eat candy in the car, then did not pay attention as he did so."

She appreciated that he had faith in her, but at the end, Pia wasn't sure that mattered. "Kids are unpredictable," she said. "It's impossible to know when an emergency might arise. I managed in the car with Paolo, but look what happened when he went running in the fountain. I panicked. And when Arturo jumped out of that swing, I didn't even move to help. I was so scared, I was completely useless."

Noise from the palace entrance floated into the rotunda, causing both Pia and Federico to turn. King Eduardo's voice rose above the low hum. Pia couldn't pick out the words, but it sounded like a greeting. Pia realized that Antony, Jennifer, and the king had finished with the press and that the guests were starting to arrive.

"Listen," she began, "we don't have much time to discuss this. Bottom line is, I don't know if I can ever get comfortable enough around children to stay, even if I didn't already have a commitment to my job. And you can do better than an accident-prone blonde who goes into panic mode whenever she sees a kid do the things kids normally do. I care for you enough to want the best for you, and for your sons. I want you to be happy."

The creases across Federico's brow deepened, and he shook his head. "You are what is best for me, and for the boys. You are stronger than you think. What happened with Arturo should have scared you. It scared me, and he was on a *swing*, of all things. Then, when Paolo played his prank in the fountain, you did react. You pulled him out of the water immediately. I saw the entire event, and Paolo was only away from your side for three or four seconds. Not long enough for harm to have come to him. You even told me afterward that you were sure he hadn't been out of your reach long enough to suffer any harm."

"Still—"

"Still, when it counted—when Paolo was choking—you acted as any medical professional might. You stayed calm, you removed him from his seat, put him in a position that allowed you to work on him, and you saved his life."

Federico glanced past her, toward the sound of his father and Antony's voices, which were moving closer.

Pia pulled away from the prince and stood, trying not to wobble in her unfamiliar high heels. "I'm glad Paolo's all right, and not just because of the confidence boost it gives me. But Federico, I can't conquer a lifetime of misgivings in a single day. My flight to Africa is tonight. I need to be on it."

He rose beside her, then caressed her cheeks, forcing her to look him in the eye as he spoke. In a whisper, he pleaded, "Take the time to discover your capabilities. Take the time to discover what we have."

Pia tried not to breathe, knowing that even a hint of his warm, clean scent filling her senses would send her over the edge, though his hands and his gaze alone threatened to do it.

"What about my job? I can't just walk away. People are counting on me."

"Let's talk about it."

A split second before the others entered the rotunda, he took her by the hand and led her up the staircase. She ascended faster than she thought possible, given her heels, but they were soon at the top and out of sight of the royal family below. They passed a security guard, who merely nodded at Federico as if seeing him holding a woman's hand and speeding down a hallway was an everyday occurrence. In less than a minute, he reached a door with a keypad and tapped in a code.

"This is my apartment," he said as they entered. "We have at least a half hour before all the guests are inside, and another fifteen to thirty minutes of cocktails before everyone is seated for lunch. If we are back by the end of the cocktail hour, we should be fine."

Once they passed through the vestibule, she took in the space. In all her weeks at La Rocca, she hadn't been inside Federico's private apartment. Floor to ceiling windows dominated one side of the room, bathing the space in sunlight. A seating area with comfortable-looking sofas and two chairs were angled to face a large, flat-screen television. To one side of the television, a door led to what appeared to be a compact kitchen. To the other side, a door opened on a hall-way. She imagined the boys' rooms and Federico's room were there.

"It's more modern than Antony and Jennifer's apartment," she said. What she didn't say was that she'd imagined Federico, Prince Perfect himself, would have a more traditional space that included some of his family's antique pieces. Instead, the decor was simple, with few knickknacks.

"Lucrezia had it redone after Arturo was born so he would have more space to play, and so the television would be easy to see. We had nicer rugs and furniture, but decided to put them in storage until the boys were older. All the fine art pieces were put in storage, as well."

"Smart."

"I was not certain I would like it, but I do. It is more relaxing." He guided her to one of the sofas, then said, "About your job. I under-stand that you made a commitment and you take it as seriously as I take mine. But talk to Jennifer about your options. She no longer spends her time in camps helping refugees, but she makes a real difference with her charity work. She made a transition, but did not rush it. She and Antony dated long distance for a while. Perhaps we could try that, too."

She remembered Jennifer's experience well. During those months, Jennifer set aside time most nights to make quick calls to Antony from their camp. He also made several visits. Their relationship deep-ened during that time, but Jennifer never abandoned her post. She did what she had committed to do, while considering new ways to help others.

Federico continued, "Your experience in the world, having spent time in isolated locations in a way someone in my position never can, makes all the difference in your ability to raise awareness about a cause. Just think what would happen if you could combine your experience with the resources here at La Rocca to help others understand the extent of the HIV epidemic in Africa."

He slid closer, then ran one hand along her arm. "What I'm trying to say is that if you wish to honor your commitment in Africa, I understand. We could build a relationship and handle it as Jennifer and Antony did, if you desire. On the other hand, a selfish part of me wants to insist that you stay. I worry that if you go, you might not return. That distance will make you question yourself, and you will use the job to hide from your fears."

Federico's words struck a chord deep within her, causing her to pull back a fraction.

Had she used her job to hide? She'd freely admitted to herself years ago that she'd used it to escape her mother. When she'd graduated college and her mother began hinting she should return to San Rimini to seek employment, she'd jumped on the chance to join an aid organization. It allowed her to help people and avoid Sabrina at the same time.

But had the job also been an excuse to escape *life?* Her friends graduated, started jobs, and eventually started families. For someone in her profession, where she might be on duty around the clock, and could be called upon to transfer to a new location on short notice, pursuing a romance had posed a great challenge. That, in turn, meant little risk of children.

She'd kept herself so busy she'd never had to face the issue. Nor had anyone questioned it before Federico.

All at once, she knew he was right. The assignments she'd accepted had kept her from being directly responsible for children. At Haffali, where she worked with Jennifer, she'd been around children throughout the day, but there had been medical staff, counselors, and in many cases one or both parents who shouldered the caregiving and responsibility. She had made troubleshooting her specialty, ensuring that supplies were acquired and distributed, that water was protected, and that camp facilities remained in good condition.

She'd taken on those roles with a passion. She'd also hidden behind them.

"How is it that you know more about me than I do?"

He continued to run his hand along her arm, moving in the slow, caring way of a longtime lover. What struck Pia as odd was that it didn't feel odd. It felt comforting. And right.

He shrugged, a soft smile on his face. "We have much in common. Your job satisfies you, but in many ways, it has provided the means to avoid what frightens you. Thinking about your situation has made me realize that my position has served the same role."

At her look of confusion, he said, "I told you at the hospital that I never loved Lucrezia. When I proposed to her, I believed it was for the right reasons. One must only look at the Windsors to understand how I convinced myself that marrying Lucrezia—a friend who would never embarrass me, and who was willing to become a textbook royal spouse—was the logical thing to do. I knew my parents would never question my decision. Lucrezia was intelligent, beautiful, poised, and from a family with a reputation for kindness and charity."

"But—?"

"We understood each other, and I called it love. It was not. It was comfortable. I used my position to justify my decision, but in truth, I married Lucrezia for other reasons. I wanted to avoid having my heart broken. I knew if she married me, she would be loyal. And I never wanted my romantic life to become the focus of media speculation or scandal. I did not believe love or romance was worth ruining either my mental equilibrium or my reputation."

He shook his head, and Pia realized he was straining to contain his emotions. "It took losing Lucrezia— and finding you—to realize how rewarding, how transforming it can be. How worthwhile. Now that I have discovered it, I do not wish to let the opportunity go. I do not wish to let you go."

She closed her eyes, allowing herself a moment to think. Federico was a planner, but he was also perceptive. What he said made sense. It made her see that the pinprick of light that represented a hope they might be together was slowly opening, becoming larger.

Becoming possible.

She savored his touch for another long moment, then opened her eyes. "You're willing to sacrifice your reputation to have a relationship with me?"

"I am. But I do not believe I have to."

"You yourself said you wanted to honor Lucrezia. If we were to begin a relationship—even if we take things very slowly—you know what will show up in the media. It will be just like the hospital. People will make assumptions, publish them, and call them facts."

She put a hand on top of his, where he still traced a path along her arm. This was the hard part. "Even if the media isn't a problem, I could still break your heart. I'm not perfect. I will make mistakes. And we haven't known each other long. We still have a lot to discover."

"What if I told you I am willing to take the chance? And that I am far from perfect, no matter what nicknames the media might give me." He smiled. "If you are willing to do this, so am I."

A laugh escaped her. "Do this? You make it sound like we're accepting a dare."

"We are." He shrugged. "It is a dare I wish to take."

She leaned forward, and he met her partway, capturing her mouth for a slow, tender kiss, one full of promise. She smiled against him, then pulled back enough to lift one hand to his chest, then slide it to his shoulder, before raising her eyes to his. Hope, desire, and anticipation were all evident in his expression, and it made her heart trip.

"I will still be on that plane tonight. For the next few months, I will be traveling a lot. I'm making stops in at least four countries, and will be in some places longer than others, depending on the need. There will be days I won't have phone or Internet. But I promise, I'll be back to San Rimini. I don't know how often or when, but I will be back. If you're willing to wait."

"I am not going anywhere," he said, and the rough note in his voice nearly undid her.

"I'll know my schedule in the next few days and can plan times to talk to you. I'd love to talk to the boys, too, if you're comfortable with that."

He nodded, then closed his eyes. His hands went to her waist. His hold was firm. He was done talking.

So was she.

This time, when their mouths met, tenderness quickly gave way to heat. His hands slid to her waist, then her hips. When Pia pulled at his suit jacket, he tossed it over the nearby chair, then his touch returned in an instant, his hands framing her ribcage before moving higher. He exhaled when his knuckles grazed her breasts through her dress.

She wanted to hold him to her as close as possible. To climb into his lap, to wrap her arms around his broad shoulders, and to stay here in his apartment until they fell asleep.

Federico's thoughts must have taken the same track, because he murmured near her ear, "At the very most, we have thirty-five minutes."

Her response was to turn her mouth to his and intensify their kiss. A sound of satisfaction rose from Federico, and his grip on her tightened. His hands moved higher, one cradling her breast while the other moved along her side. Each touch, each breath, each moment made her more and more certain she was making the right decision.

She could love this man. She could love him for life. He was worth fighting demons for.

Federico's hand stilled when his thumb encountered the pull on the dress's hidden side zipper.

She broke their kiss and said, "Yes."

Before she could kiss him again, he eased back. "If I do this, I won't want to stop until the moment we must return to the reception."

"I won't want to stop, either." She smiled and added, "and you just used another contraction."

"I must be comfortable with you."

She raked her hands into his hair. "Then go ahead."

Instead of pulling the zipper, he lifted her to stand, held her hand, and walked her to his bedroom. Before she could take in the layout, he hit a button near the door that dropped a set of shades. They didn't black out the room, but let in filtered light. He used his heel to close the bedroom door as he reached for her.

"We might not have much time, but we can do better than my sitting room sofa."

Despite his warning about the time, he drew the zipper slowly, then helped her step out of the dress. He caught it as it fell, then lay it across a chair. "We can enjoy this without returning in wrinkled clothing."

She followed his lead, undressing him with care, allowing him to lay each piece of clothing beside her dress. All the while, he kissed her temples, her cheeks, her shoulders. When he wore nothing but his underwear, he walked her to the bed.

The emotion on his face melted her heart. In that moment, she knew he'd truly believed he'd never have a woman in his bed again, and that for him, this was a transformative experience.

She stroked his chest with one hand, feeling the texture of the fine, dark hair that covered layers of muscle. It didn't take long to find the thrum of his heart. "I wish we had more time."

"As long as there is a next time, we have more time."

"There will be a next time." It was a solemn promise. His arms came around her, and in his kiss, she felt him make the promise, too.

They sank to the bed, mouths and limbs entwined. The pressure of his body against hers was heaven. Anything she could have daydreamed about making love to Federico paled in comparison to what it felt like to have him caress and kiss every conceivable spot on her body. When he took one nipple in his mouth, she sighed in response. She was already hot and wet and ready for him, but he continued to explore and tantalize, bringing her within moments of orgasm, then easing the stimulation before driving her mad once more in an exquisite cycle. Finally, he reached for his nightstand. Then, with a grimace, withdrew his hand and closed his eyes.

"I don't have anything...anything to—"

She pressed a kiss to his forehead. "I am on birth control and I'm completely healthy. I have regular physicals for work. I get tested for everything under the sun, given where I travel."

"Are you certain?"

"If you are. I trust you."

"I love you, Pia Renati. I would not have believed it when I met you at the airport and you held that book—"

"Oh, don't remind me."

"But you are exactly the person I want and need in my life."

As she kissed him, a single hot tear ran down her cheek. She knew that Federico diTalora would be the best decision she ever made. They'd each avoided love, avoided the risk of heartbreak. But those years of avoidance meant that when they were faced with the real thing, they recognized it.

When he entered her at last, her breath caught. His hand reached for hers, interlacing their fingers. She exhaled, then they began to move. When he shuddered above her, she lifted and kissed the pulse at his throat. Moments later, she came apart, her body trembling and her heart pounding. Then Federico's arms were around her.

She was in the right place. With the right man.

A perfectly imperfect man.

PIA AND FEDERICO slipped into the rotunda together. Guests surrounded the king, Antony and Jennifer, and the baby, all vying for a chance to see Prince Gianluca and to be seen with the diTaloras. Nick and Isabella spoke to a group of guests from the nearby university, where Nick was on the faculty, while Amanda chatted with Helena Masciaretti, the sister of the late queen. Marco was engaged in conversation with a group of Antony's friends, including Pia's cousin, Angelo. Only a few people mingling near the side hallway they used to make their entrance noticed their late arrival.

"I should have known Angelo would be here," Pia said. "You know what he'll think."

"Does it matter?"

"No." She gave him a discreet smile. "If he says something, I'll point out that I'm not wrinkled."

Federico's mouth twisted into a wicked grin. They'd had to clean up quickly, but a check in the mirror before they left his apartment made Pia confident no one would guess what had taken place.

A woman with an expensive-looking camera wove in and out of

the guests, discreetly capturing the event. Most of the shots would stay in the family's private collection, but Pia knew that the palace's public relations office would release several to the press, and that they would appear on the evening news or in tomorrow's papers. After shooting several of the VIPs in attendance, the photographer paused near Jennifer. When Jennifer finished speaking with the man beside her, the photographer leaned in and said something in her ear. Jennifer nodded, then turned and walked directly toward Pia and Federico. Gianluca was nestled in her arms. She didn't say anything about the fact they'd missed the bulk of the cocktail hour, but Pia could tell from the quick flash in Jennifer's eyes that she was dying to ask.

Instead, she smiled and said, "We missed getting shots of you at the Duomo with Gianluca. Do you mind? The lighting is better here in the rotunda than inside the Imperial Ballroom."

Pia smiled at the prince and, feeling like a cliff diver about to take a dangerous leap into unknown waters, she nodded.

Jennifer eased Gianluca from her arms into Federico's. "I'd like photos of each of you holding him, if that's all right."

Federico looked at Pia, but told Jennifer, "I believe we could be persuaded."

The photographer moved them to stand near the staircase. They posed for several photos with Federico holding the baby before it was Pia's turn. He turned to face her. "Ready?"

"As long as you're here."

"I am not going anywhere." Federico's face split into a wide grin just before he leaned over the baby and kissed her cheek.

She should have been shocked, but somehow, she wasn't. Pia smiled, then, very carefully, she took the tiny bundle into her arms. Little Luc was warm and smelled of love, and he blinked up at her with hazy blue eyes.

"You are okay?" Federico asked, and she understood that he was talking about the baby, rather than the kiss.

"Yes." As they turned to face the camera, she added, "he's wonderful."

"I don't believe I shall be called 'Prince Perfect' any longer," he whispered, his words barely audible over the conversation surrounding them as the photographer shifted to take photos from a new angle. "I just started the gossip mill turning."

"It doesn't matter," she whispered. "You're *my* Prince Perfect. I plan to remind you every day."

EPILOGUE

Three Years Later

"I STILL DON'T KNOW a placenta previa from a placenta accreta," Pia told Federico, careful to keep Arturo and Paolo from hearing her as she stood behind them at their dining room table and helped Arturo with his school project.

"I do not think it will matter." Federico lightly touched his hand to her lower back, then leaned forward to brush the top of her head with a kiss. "If it does, we will learn together."

"Mamma, you told me it isn't polite to whisper," Paolo said, frowning at her.

"You're right. I'm setting a bad example." She winked at Paolo, who now reminded her so much of Arturo at that age, back when she'd first met the boys and they'd struck her with the boomerang. Paolo had grown into a confident, bright boy who loved his friends, his school, and his new dog.

Pia couldn't be more thrilled that both boys had started to call her Mamma. She and Federico had taken things slowly, dating long distance at first. She gradually spent more and more time with the boys, letting them see the nature of the work she did for HIV awareness and education.

They'd married nearly two years after Gianluca's christening. It had been a quiet ceremony in the palace's private chapel, attended by immediate family, and was exactly the type of wedding Pia wanted. It had suited Federico and the boys, too.

She hoped Lucrezia would have approved. Though she'd only met Federico's first wife briefly during Jennifer and Antony's wedding, she felt she owed Lucrezia a great debt. Before the wedding ceremony, Pia had entered the chapel alone, lifted her face skyward, and promised Lucrezia that she would protect her children, always.

"Your mother is setting an excellent example," Federico said as he accepted the paper Arturo held out for proofreading. "The children at the AIDS shelter in Zimbabwe will be excited to receive all the letters from you and your classmates."

"And my pictures," Paolo added, holding up a watercolor painting that Pia guessed was of Paolo himself. "Will we get to visit them again soon?"

Pia and Federico's gazes met, and a secret smile passed between them.

"Mamma might not be able to travel to Zimbabwe for a little while, Paolo," Federico told him. "She is working on an important project here."

"What kind of project?" Arturo straightened in his chair and set down his pencil. "Is it for the children?"

Pia grinned, recalling the gift Federico had given her the night before—a yellow, floral-jacketed pregnancy book, along with a brand-spanking new copy of *The Laid-Back Mom's Guide to Baby's First Year*, third edition. She told Arturo, "It involves children, yes, but—"

"It's in the early stages," Federico finished. "We shall tell you more about Mamma's project later, all right? For now, we should organize this mess. Your new nanny will arrive at any moment to take you to the movies."

"You *finally* found a nanny, Papa?" Paolo asked. "Mamma said she didn't think you'd ever find one."

"I didn't," Pia admitted. "But I know a wonderful woman who recently retired, and she tells me that all her life she's wanted nothing more than to care for children. Now she has the chance."

Arturo's eyes brightened. "It's Grandma Sabrina, isn't it?"

Pia gestured toward the table. "Clean up quick, or you'll never know, will you?"

"It is!" Both boys cheered and vacated their seats. As they scrambled to clean up the mess, Federico leaned close to Pia and whispered, "Once they leave, we shall celebrate in private."

"We're supposed to attend Nick and Isabella's fundraiser for the museum's medieval art exhibition. It's in an hour."

"Then we shall be late."

"You can't get me—you know—when I'm already—"

"It would be fun to try, though."

She raised an eyebrow, then skirted the table to help the boys tidy their projects. "If you insist, Your Highness."

"Oh, I do," he assured her, reaching across the table to hold her hand and run his fingers over her gold wedding band. "I'll even make sure you arrive unwrinkled."

She laughed. The man was perfect.

Thank you for reading *Falling for Prince Federico*. If you enjoyed this book, please consider leaving a review at your favorite bookstore or book club website.

Learn about Nicole's upcoming releases and receive special insider bonuses by subscribing to her newsletter at nicoleburnham.com.

Read on for an excerpt from the next Royal Scandals: San Rimini story, the all-new novel *To Kiss a King*, which features King Eduardo diTalora and Claire Peyton, the new United States Ambassador to San Rimini.

TO KISS A KING

Chapter One

"Good morning, Your Highness. How was your time with Greta this morning?"

King Eduardo diTalora cast a sidelong glance at his longtime personal assistant, Luisa Borelli, as she fell into step beside him. Polished as always, she wore a soft brown skirt and tailored jacket with low heels. Her black hair was twisted into a flawless knot at her nape and tiny gold studs dotted her earlobes.

Luisa was very good at her job. One would never know by looking at her that she was also the devil incarnate.

Eduardo shook his head, then looked forward, his smile encompassing various staff members who lingered in the hallway, waiting for him to arrive at his office. To Luisa, he said, "It wouldn't be a proper Monday morning if Greta hadn't spent the weekend plotting new ways to torture me."

"Precisely which part of the session did you find torturous, Your Highness? The box jumps?"

"No, because she decided to change the box jump portion of the workout to stepping onto the box—"

"Oh, good—"

"While holding a fifteen-kilo medicine ball."

"Oh."

"Then she added a series of planks. Apparently, running is insufficient for building core strength. I attempted to convince her otherwise, but she refused to listen to my wisdom."

"She is stubborn that way. But I daresay, Sir, when it comes to matters of health and fitness, Greta is usually right."

"As is the cousin who referred her and wouldn't stop nagging me until I hired her." He raised a brow at Luisa, but buffered it with a smile that she returned.

Eduardo wished one of the guards a good morning as he and Luisa rounded the final corner to his office, then Luisa said, "It's my duty to ensure you serve the country to the best of your ability. Maintaining a high level of fitness is essential to that task. If it makes you feel better, tomorrow I've scheduled a run at six a.m. The weather should be ideal. Mild and clear with low wind."

Most people would consider a sunrise run torture, but to Eduardo, a crack of dawn jaunt along San Rimini's waterfront or through the hills above the palace sounded like heaven. He could breathe fresh air, listen to music, and allow his mind to wander. For that single hour, he was responsible to no one but himself, and there was no Greta at his side to insist he could work harder or crank out one more rep.

If he could crank out one more rep, he was the type to do so without being told.

Eduardo greeted a courier who waited near Luisa's desk, then glanced at his assistant. "I'd be obliged if there are waffles in the dining room following that run tomorrow. Samuel had oatmeal today. Good oatmeal, but still oatmeal."

"I'll see what I can do, though Samuel mentioned that he's planning on baked quinoa with berries."

"I'll pretend I didn't hear that."

"Perhaps you could pretend it's a waffle?"

"I shall pretend I didn't hear that, either. I'll pretend you said, 'Yes,

Your Highness, I will request waffles and ensure Samuel provides plenty of syrup. Perhaps a few of those berries on the side.'"

Luisa raised a finger to indicate that the courier should wait for her, then she and Eduardo entered his formal office. Eduardo's chief political advisor, Sergio Ribisi, sat on a sofa beside Eduardo's press secretary, a burly young man named Zeno Amendola who looked better suited to commanding a rugby team than a press room. The two were hunched over a tablet, reviewing what Eduardo assumed were notes for their morning meeting. Across from them sat Margaret Halaby, his Director of Charities and Patronages. Margaret had her hands in her lap, a pen threaded between her fingers. A notepad lay across on the sofa beside her, its top page filled with indiscernible scribbles, bullet points, and arrows. She stared past the two men, lost in thought.

Luisa made a small noise to catch their attention. All three rose in unison and wished Eduardo a good morning. He waved them back into their seats, then asked Luisa to give him a five-minute warning before he needed to leave for his first event of the day.

"How was your session with Greta?" Zeno asked once Luisa closed the door behind her.

He nailed Zeno with a glare. The man had the audacity to grin in return.

"I saw her carrying a medicine ball through the parking garage," Margaret said. She turned to Zeno. "Ever do squats with one of those? Or throw them at a target? It makes for a fantastic workout."

"Medicine balls are great tools." He widened his eyes in mock excitement. "I like to do walking lunges while holding one overhead. Real muscle burner."

"This is a conspiracy," Eduardo told them. "I can outrun everyone in this building except the security personnel—and perhaps even a few of them—yet all of you insist I see Greta three times a week."

"It's reassuring to the citizens of San Rimini to know that you are taking steps to protect your health and that your heart is as strong as can be following your surgery," Sergio said. "Besides, you like Greta."

"Not when she's telling me to hold a side plank an extra thirty seconds. I informed her that San Rimini has strict laws against injuring the monarch."

"I'm sure she reminded you that you signed a waiver?" Zeno retorted.

He eyed his press secretary. "She insisted that she wasn't injuring the monarch. *Then* she informed me that it didn't matter because I'd signed a waiver."

Eduardo took a seat at his desk, then thanked Luisa as she reentered the room with a steaming cup of coffee and placed it on a coaster near his hand. When she was gone again, he looked at Sergio. The arrival of Eduardo's first cup of coffee marked the official start of his workday. "Let's discuss the difficult items first. You received a letter over the weekend from the Central District Historical Society?"

"Yes, Your Highness. They have concerns about your desire to upgrade the Strada il Teatro."

"I expected as much, but hoped they would wait until tomorrow's meeting to express them."

"They want to ensure they are heard."

Eduardo resisted the urge to grimace. Everyone wanted to be heard, particularly when it came to making changes to the country's most famous thoroughfare. The Strada il Teatro sat above the country's Adriatic coastline and offered stunning views of San Rimini Bay. It was home to several casinos, restaurants, historical buildings, and the Royal Theater, hence its name as Theater Street. It was the country's most recognizable symbol, aside from the Duomo and the palace itself. However, the last major changes to the street—aside from paving it—took place long before automobiles were commonplace. Traffic often moved at a crawl and the sidewalks were packed with tourists at all hours. Despite the obvious need for refurbishment, San Riminians were protective of its appearance. It was why Sergio had organized a meeting for the following day to present the king's proposal to those most directly affected. He'd invited representatives from the Central District Historical Society, the casino owners' board, the San Rimini Business Council, and the San Rimini Grand Prix organizing committee, together with the country's transportation minister. Sergio had even included those in charge of maintaining the public park that ran below one section of the Strada. Once Sergio had their buy in, Eduardo planned to present a comprehensive modernization plan to Parliament for their consideration.

As king of San Rimini, Eduardo had more power to affect policy than monarchs in countries such as Japan or Sweden. He could not vote, but he had the right to introduce legislation and speak to any matter under discussion in Parliament. In the centuries since San Rimini had transitioned from an absolute monarchy to a constitutional monarchy, kings and queens primarily exercised their political might to improve relations with other nations or to promote charitable and humanitarian causes. They steered clear of detailed policy and budgetary issues.

This piece of legislation would cause many to dig in their heels. However, Eduardo refused to leave the modernization to his successors or to members of parliament who feared that touching the Strada il Teatro meant losing their seats. It was his responsibility to move San Rimini forward.

Eduardo looked at Sergio. "Inform the head of the Historical Society that the palace fully intends to pursue these improvements—make sure you use that word, improvements—to the Strada il Teatro, as they're in the best interest of the country and to all who hold the central district close to their hearts. We welcome their input tomorrow, which is why we've scheduled this meeting."

Sergio nodded as he took notes. While Sergio wrote, Zeno said, "Your Highness, they're likely to argue their case to the press. They'll note that it isn't in the monarch's usual purview to delve into such matters."

Eduardo spread his palms on his desk. "As of last week, I understand that the royal family is viewed favorably by nearly eighty percent of the population."

"Seventy-seven percent, sir."

"Seventy-seven percent. Do you know how many members of parliament dream of that approval rating? We have the opportunity to leverage that number for the long-term good of the country. The

Strada has remained essentially the same for hundreds of years. The fact it was constructed with parades in mind means it's wider than other streets of its era, but it doesn't accommodate modern usage or the influx of tourism our country has seen. Attendees at the San Rimini Grand Prix are pushing against the fences, which is a safety concern. Either the route will need to change or we will need to limit the crowds. No one wants to make that choice."

"Everyone has their fiefdoms," Sergio pointed out. "The casinos and shop owners don't want their entrances blocked while work is completed. The Historical Society doesn't want to alter the appearance of the street. And while the Grand Prix organizers want a safer route and continued growth, they don't want to risk losing the race for a year or more due to construction."

"Agreed," Eduardo said. "So use tomorrow to show them our redevelopment plan, and use our historical and transportation experts to convince them that our proposal is sound. We've put months of research into this, and we're willing to share all of our findings and to listen to their input as we move forward. Change is difficult, but our citizens need the Strada to function for the long term. If we don't get it through parliament with a seventy-seven percent approval rating, we'll never get it. Now, what else do we need to address?"

Zeno ran through the items he would cover at the weekly press briefing, which mainly involved the king's adult children. Prince Antony had visited an opioid addiction rehabilitation facility over the weekend, and Princess Isabella and her husband, Nick, planned to visit three different schools along the country's northern border to talk with students about San Rimini's medieval history. Nick, a medieval studies professor at the University of San Rimini, had arranged a string of school appearances in recent weeks to interest children in the topic.

When Zeno finished, Sergio said, "Tomorrow night, you are hosting a dinner at which the new American ambassador shall present her credentials. She arrived in country yesterday."

"Claire Peyton," Eduardo said, leaning back in his chair. "I read the briefing last night. She was previously the United States Ambassador to Uganda?"

"Yes. It was expected that she would stay on under the new President, but she was reassigned to San Rimini when Ambassador Cartwright announced his retirement." Sergio paused. "It's not a secret that Rich Cartwright spent his final year or two on cruise control. This will be a change. Given that many in the U.S. State Department consider this an elevation of position, she may wish to prove herself."

"I read about the rural education program she helped institute in Uganda. It looked interesting."

"Yes, Your Highness. She will likely request a meeting in the coming weeks to present it to you and ask for San Rimini's involvement. The American president ran on a campaign that focused heavily on education, so it's a priority for the administration. However, it's ultimately a no go for San Rimini. Parliament might support sending funds, but sending teachers or advisors would be less likely, given current security concerns. Even the funds will be a challenge while we're also trying to push the Strada plan."

Eduardo didn't need time to weigh his priorities. There was no contest. "It's my understanding that parliament will address funding for Central District improvements three months from today. I want our proposal to anchor that discussion. From now until then, that's our focus."

He took a sip of his coffee, then asked Margaret, "Where are we on the Our Place program?"

"The five-year anniversary celebration will take place on Friday at the elementary school on Via Fontana. As Patron, you will speak briefly about the need for early intervention mental health support in schools and highlight the ways that Our Place identifies and assists children without stigmatizing them. I have some statistics on the continued need for the program and on its success. I should have a draft speech to you by Thursday, which you can then adapt to your liking."

"Thank you. That's a visit I look forward to making. Any others?"

Margaret ran through updates on two other charitable organizations the king supported, then provided a follow-up report on an event he'd attended for an animal shelter.

At the same moment Margaret finished her update, Luisa entered the room. "Your ride is waiting, Your Highness. Your tour of the dementia care center begins in twenty minutes."

Eduardo thanked Luisa and stood. Sergio, Zeno, and Margaret stood as well. "Are we finished?"

"One last thing, Your Highness," Zeno said. "There will be questions at today's press briefing regarding your visit to the Duomo this Thursday afternoon. Have you decided whether to deliver any remarks?"

Eduardo felt the corner of his mouth twitch, a dead giveaway to his staff that he was uncomfortable with a topic. It was a tell he could usually control, but this had hit him out of the blue. Somehow, between his morning workout and thoughts about the Strada, he'd forgotten his annual trip to visit his wife's final resting place.

"Next year will be the tenth anniversary of Queen Aletta's death. Given the attention that occasion will draw, I'd prefer to skip the remarks this year and keep the visit low key."

Before Zeno could object, he turned to Luisa and asked, "Do I have any free time this afternoon to see Arturo and Paolo when they get home from school?"

The boys, sons of Prince Federico and his late wife, Lucrezia, were always happy when he appeared at their palace apartment for a visit. He refused to consider whether their smiles were due to his sparkling personality or to the treats he often brought from the kitchen.

"Not today," Luisa said. "They have a school trip to the aquarium and won't return until evening."

"I see. And what about time to see Gianluca?" he asked. Prince Antony and his wife Jennifer's infant son was his newest grandchild. "Does anyone know when the baby sleeps?"

A chorus of *no* and *he doesn't* rose around the room.

"Well, then. Please let Jennifer know that if there's a good time, I'd love to visit. If Gianluca happens to be sleeping, I'll simply watch him sleep."

"You have fifteen minutes free around three-thirty, Your Highness. I'll let her know you'll be available."

He nodded to Luisa, thanked Margaret for the work she was doing on the Our Place speech, then addressed Sergio and Zeno. "You know what to do for the Strada. We have ninety days. Let's improve the country."

ALSO BY NICOLE BURNHAM

ROYAL SCANDALS

Christmas With a Prince (prequel novella)

Scandal With a Prince

Honeymoon With a Prince

Christmas on the Royal Yacht (novella)

Slow Tango With a Prince

The Royal Bastard

Christmas With a Palace Thief (novella)

The Wicked Prince

One Man's Princess

ROYAL SCANDALS: SAN RIMINI

Fit for a Queen

Going to the Castle

The Prince's Tutor

The Knight's Kiss

Falling for Prince Federico

To Kiss a King

BOWEN, NEBRASKA

The Bowen Bride

A ROYAL SCANDALS WEDDING

More Royal Scandals titles will be available soon. For updates, please visit nicoleburnham.com, where you can subscribe to Nicole's Newsletter.

Subscribers receive exclusive content, including the short story *A Royal Scandals Wedding*, an inside look at the wedding of Megan Hallberg and Prince Stefano Barrali from the novel Scandal With a Prince.

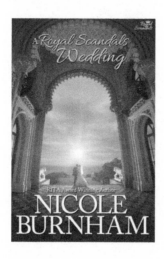

ABOUT THE AUTHOR

 Nicole Burnham is the RITA award-winning author of over twenty novels, including the popular Royal Scandals series.

Nicole graduated from an American high school in Germany, then obtained a BA in political science from Colorado State University and a JD/MA from the University of Michigan. She lives near Boston, spends as much time as possible at Fenway Park, and travels abroad whenever she can score cheap airfare.

Readers may visit Nicole's website and subscribe to her newsletter at nicoleburnham.com.

facebook.com/NicoleBurnhamBooks
twitter.com/NicoleBurnham
instagram.com/nicole.burnham

Made in the USA
Las Vegas, NV
29 April 2022

48208270R00100